TALES FROM BRAEMORE

SWEIN ASLEIFSON – A NORTHERN PIRATE

Tales from Braemore & Swein Asleifson
A Northern Pirate

Robert P. Gunn

Whittles Publishing

Published by
Whittles Publishing Ltd.,
Dunbeath,
Caithness, KW6 6EG,
Scotland, UK
www.whittlespublishing.com

combined edition © 2018 Whittles Publishing
drawings by Barbara Myatt

All rights reserved.
No part of this publication may be reproduced,
stored in a retrieval system, or transmitted,
in any form or by any means, electronic,
mechanical, recording or otherwise
without prior permission of the publishers.

Kind thanks to the McPherson and Plowman
families for the use of their photographs.

ISBN 978-184995-276-7

Printed by

Contents

Tales from Braemore

Who Discovered America? 1
A Legend of Loch More 6
The Beauty of Braemore 12
The Prisoner's Leap 19
The Giant of Morven 28
Graysteel the Robber of Loch Rangag 34
The Dairymaid and the Hunter 42
The Writing on the Wall 49
The Battle of Altimarlach 52
John Finlaison 59
The Strong Man of Dalnaglaton 65
David Marshall, the Backlass Robber 70
The Snowstorm 75
A Fight at the Market 80
The Secret of Garrywhin 83
Recollections of School Days at Badbea 85
The Last Need Fire 94
Bloodshed at Berriedale 97
Excise Men and Smugglers 99
The Leodibest Battle 102

Swein Asleifson
A Northern Pirate

Courage and Treachery in a 12th Century Viking Adventure 106

v

Tales from Braemore

PREFACE

IN CAITHNESS, BEFORE THE ADVENT of television, during the long winter nights, people used to hold informal gatherings in each other's houses, and spend the night in general conversation around the firesides. These gatherings were known as ceilidhs. The news of the day was always discussed along with other topics of interest. Invariably the conversation would turn to events of long ago and it was then that the story tellers came into their own.

Over the years I have collected these legends and historical articles as a hobby as I have always believed that they should be preserved. I have written them down in a similar manner to the way in which they were told at the ceilidhs. Some of them have been published in the *Scots Magazine*, and are reproduced with the editor's permission. I hope that this book will give readers an insight into early life in Caithness and that they will obtain pleasure from it.

In this new edition, I have added further stories and photographs which I hope will enrich the book and transport the reader to those long-ago days.

Who Discovered America?

AT SCHOOL WE WERE TAUGHT how Christopher Columbus discovered America in 1492. This is accepted as a fact by most people but if we look back through the pages of history, information will be found which will make us doubtful if Columbus was the real discoverer. We will learn that regular voyages were being made between Greenland and North America by the Vikings in the 10th and 11th centuries. It has also been claimed that Columbus first heard of America while on a voyage to Iceland and it was information given to him by the Icelanders that led him on his voyage of rediscovery. The story of the Norse Sagas begins in 982 when a Norseman named Erik the Red, who had earlier been banished from Norway for a series of killings and now lived in Iceland, was banished from Iceland for three years for a further outbreak of killings. He was already outlawed from Norway so he decided to sail west where he believed that there was another land which had been sighted 50 years earlier by another Norwegian named Gunbjorn. Erik and his followers sailed for some time and eventually reached the coast of Greenland to the west of Cape Farewell. They did not meet any natives of Greenland so they decided to farm there.

When Erik's three-year period of banishment was over he decided to return to Iceland so that he could get men and women to come to Greenland with him to colonise it. When Erik returned to Iceland there was a famine and many of the Norse settlers were willing to come with him to settle in this new land. Twenty-five ships set out with Erik on the return journey from Iceland to Greenland.

The first sighting of America by a European was not planned. The first man to do so was an Icelander named Bjarni Herjolfsson. He had spent the winter of 985-986 in Norway and the following summer intended to return to Iceland and spend the winter with his father, Herjolf. He set sail for Iceland with a full cargo, but when he arrived there he found that his father had sold his estates in Iceland and had departed for Greenland on a colonising expedition with Erik the Red. Bjarni was determined to follow his father so he collected all the information that he could gather about Greenland and then set out for it without any navigational aids to help him.

He sailed for three days from Iceland towards Greenland when north winds overtook him and after the winds abated a thick fog settled on the sea and he had no idea which way he was going. When the sun eventually broke through, he took fresh bearings, hoisted a sail and sailed on what he thought was the direction for Greenland, before he saw land. The land was full of forests and had low hills so he knew that this was not Greenland for which he had been heading.

Bjarni was still determined in his own mind that this was a part of Greenland so he turned north along the coast and sailed for two days. The land he saw was still full of forests and very flat. Bjarni still decided not to land as he was uncertain if this was Greenland so he turned away from from the land and sailed for four days before a strong wind until he reached Greenland. Bjarni without knowing it had been sailing along the coast of North America.

Fifteen years later, a Norseman named Leif Eriksson, a son of Erik the Red, set out on a voyage of discovery from Greenland. He bought Bjarni Herjolfsson's ship and also engaged some of his crew who had been on the original voyage of discovery. Leif sailed to Baffin Island and landed there. He also made voyages to Labrador and the northern tip of Newfoundland which he named Vinland. He spent the winter in Newfoundland where he found that the days were longer than in Greenland. Leif returned to Greenland the next summer and was full of praise for this new land which he had discovered. His father, Erik the

Red, had died, and Leif being the oldest son was forced to take over his position so he had to give up sailing.

There has been a lot of controversy as to which part of America Leif gave the name of Vinland (or Wineland as it was said that wild grapes grew there). Several historians believed that it was the area called New England, but it now appears that it was Newfoundland as the remains of a Norse settlement has been found there. It is also believed that the temperature in Newfoundland in the 11th century was much higher than it is today and grapes could have been grown there.

Leif's brother Thorvald immediately came forward with a new plan for exploring this new country. He sailed the known route to Newfoundland and then sent some of his ships to explore the west coast. Thorvald sailed north past a cape he named Kjalarness, Keel Ness, because he lost the keel from his ship there. He then went into an inlet where he met the first natives of America who were believed to be Red Indians. Thorvald decided to attack them and in the battle which followed he was killed by an Indian arrow. Thorvald was the only person killed in the battle so his crew returned to Newfoundland. They spent the winter there and in the spring returned to Greenland.

The next significant voyage was made by a Norwegian from Iceland, named Thorfinn Karlsefni, who had sailed to Greenland with a cargo of merchandise and while there married Erik's daughter-in-law Gudrid. He set sail for Newfoundland with three ships and 160 men. Several of the men took their wives and families with them as this was believed to be an attempt to colonise the country. They also took domestic animals along with them.

After Thorfinn and his party had spent their first winter in Newfoundland, they made their first contact with the natives when a large party of men came out of the forests. At first they were frightened by the roaring of Thorfinn's bull, but when they became used to the noise they unslung their bundles and tried to trade with the Norsemen although they could not understand each other's language. The natives had skins and furs of different kinds for sale and they wished to barter them for weapons, but Thorfinn forbade any of his men to barter their weapons for skins. Instead he asked the women folk to carry out pails of milk to the natives, and when they tasted it, they decided to trade for this instead.

One morning Thorfinn and a companion named Snorri saw a number of skin boats approach the coast. The men on board were waving sticks in a sunwise motion, so Thorfinn took this as a token of peace and he held up a white shield to them. The natives recognised Thorfinn's peace motion and rowed ashore. They were small, dark-skinned men with broad cheeks and they remained ashore for a short time looking astonished at the Norsemen and then rowed away again.

Thorfinn and his men built houses for themselves near a lake and spent a second winter there. No snow fell and all their animals could graze outside. In the early spring a number of natives approached in skin boats and wished to trade with the Norsemen. Thorfinn and his party traded cloth for skins with the natives and for some time they lived in peace.

Peace, however, did not last for very long and eventually hostilities broke out between the Norsemen and the natives. Due to the lack of manpower and the difficulty of trying to get reserves from Greenland, after three winters in Newfoundland, Thorfinn decided to give up his idea of colonising the country and returned to Greenland with his party. Jealousy and ill-feeling had also broken out in his camp over the women they had brought with them.

Mention is made in the sagas of one more Norse voyage to America. This voyage was arranged by Freydis Eriksdotter, sister of Leif and Thorvald. The voyage did not meet with success and it is said to have prevented further voyages for several years. All these voyages took place before 1020 so it can be seen that the Norsemen have a strong claim to the discovery of America. It is believed that Norse voyages from Greenland to America continued until the beginning of the 13th century, but these are not recorded in the Norse sagas.

The next important voyage to America was made in 1395 by Francis Henry Sinclair, Jarl of Orkney, when he went with a large naval expedition to rediscover lands which lay far west across the Atlantic Ocean. Prince Henry was accompanied on the voyage by two Venetian noblemen, Sir Nicholas Zeno, and Sir Antonio Zeno, who were brothers. Sir Nicholas was Admiral of Prince Henry's fleet and Sir Antonio was in charge of one of the ships. The expedition first went ashore at Nova Scotia where Sir Antonio Zeno saw burning pitch running into the sea at the foot of a mountain. The expedition then sailed eastwards along the coast of Massachusetts where they stayed for some time.

Sir Antonio was sent home with part of the fleet before winter set in but Prince Henry and the remainder of his fleet spent the winter in America before returning to Scotland.

At Westford, Massachusetts, the portrait of a knight in full armour was found carved on a rock. The shield borne by the knight had carved on it a ship, and two buckles with a star in between them, which is believed to be one of the earliest examples of the coat of arms of the Clan Gunn. It is possible that the carving marks the grave of a member of the Clan Gunn who accompanied Prince Henry Sinclair on his voyage of discovery. The carving was examined by experts who revealed that it was a Norse carving of the 14th century. Prince Henry Sinclair was Jarl of Orkney and Baron of Roslin Castle in Scotland.

From the information available on these voyages to America, it appears that the Norsemen followed by the Scots were the real discoverers of America.

A Legend of Loch More

ABOUT THE BEGINNING OF THE fourteenth century, a chieftain of Norman extraction by the name of Reginald Cheyne had power over a large part of Caithness. The Cheynes were said to have come to Britain with William the Conqueror and then followed the Sinclairs on their travels to the North of Scotland. The Cheyne family first settled at Inverugie Castle in the parish of St Fergus, Aberdeenshire. They became proprietors of that parish and also had estates in Banff and Moray.

Reginald Cheyne, who settled in Caithness, was related to Henry Cheyne who was made Bishop of Aberdeen in 1281. Reginald Cheyne owned large estates in Caithness and it is said that he owned a third of the county. In addition to this he owned Castle Duffus and other estates in Moray. The castle and lands of Auldwick, Caithness, belonged to him and he often resided there. He was very fond of hunting and the chase, so he built a hunting lodge in the parish of Halkirk at the north corner of Loch More, where the river Thurso issues out of it.

Cheyne resided most of his time in this lodge with his retainers. He was a very cruel, proud and boastful man. If any of his subjects offended him, he usually put them to death. He was so proud that he openly boasted that he had power over life and death. Cheyne designed a type of trap for catching salmon which he placed in the river beside the wall of the lodge. A rope from the trap was attached to a bell in the lodge, and whenever a salmon went into the trap, the bell rang. In this way, the great Cheyne was able to announce to his guests that he had caught a salmon, even though he was seated at the dinner table.

Cheyne also sat in the Scottish Parliament, and was one of the Scottish Chiefs and Barons who drew up the Declaration of Arbroath. He also fought with the Earl of Sutherland at the disastrous battle of Halidon Hill in 1333. The Earl of Sutherland was killed and Cheyne was taken prisoner by the English. He was held prisoner for some time, and then released whereupon he returned to Caithness.

Shortly after his return from captivity he married a young lady of great beauty who was said to have been descended from one of the Norse Governors of Caithness. Cheyne had all the rich abundance of wealth that anyone could wish for, and the only thing that he really desired was for a son to inherit his wealth. At that time he resided with his wife in splendour in his lodge at Loch More. He was overjoyed when his wife announced that she was going to give birth to a child. In spite of all his worldly power and wealth, Reginald Cheyne was a very cruel man at heart and, in his eyes, a female was of little use in this type of world. Females were all right for doing housework or bearing children, but they were no use in battle, thought Cheyne. One night, while talking to his wife about the impending birth, he told her that if she gave birth to a girl he would give immediate orders for the child to be drowned in the Thurso River. His wife was horrified at his disclosure, but as she was afraid of him, she appeared to agree with his decision.

Lady Cheyne began to make secret plans in case the child turned out to be a girl. A man servant by the name of Ingram Gunn was to take the child away if it was a female and drown it. Lady Cheyne was good friends with him, and as he was a very humane man and did not want any part in the murder of a child, they devised a plan to outwit the wicked Cheyne.

Eventually, Lady Cheyne gave birth to a child, and to everyone's horror, it was a girl. Reginald Cheyne flew into a violent temper and sent for Ingram Gunn to dispose of the child. Ingram carried the child away, but quickly exchanged it with a woman from Dorrery, who had been hiding in the lodge, for a bundle of clothes which was filled with stones. The wicked Cheyne waited to hear a splash as the child drowned, and Ingram did not disappoint him. When Cheyne heard the splash by the bundle of clothes being dropped in the river, he immediately sent for Ingram Gunn, and rewarded him for doing the dastardly deed.

Meanwhile the child was being carried away over the hills to Dorrery by the woman, who brought it up as her own child. Lady Cheyne secretly saw to it that the child was well provided for.

Lady Cheyne grieved for several days on the supposed death of her child, and her husband never suspected that his plan had gone astray. Ingram Gunn was given special treatment as the great Cheyne believed that he had been his hired murderer. Cheyne was very much feared by all his servants and retainers, as they knew that if they offended him their life was at stake. Lady Cheyne, like all the other inhabitants of the lodge, feared her husband and knew her life was in danger if she did not please him.

A short time later Lady Cheyne told him that she was expecting another child. "This one must be a boy," he shouted, "or else Ingram Gunn will have to drown her like the last one. I am the proudest and richest man in this county, and surely I can say if my children are to stay alive or not."

The baby was born, and to Lady Cheyne's horror it was another girl. Reginald Cheyne flew into a violent temper and kicked all the servants who were round him. He shouted for Ingram Gunn, handed him the newborn infant, and ordered him to drown it. Ingram took the baby and hurried from the room. He handed the baby to the woman from Dorrery and picked up a bundle of clothes filled with stones. Ingram then went to a window near the room where the great Cheyne was ranting and raving and calling his wife all vile names. When Cheyne stopped shouting, Ingram dropped the bundle into the river. Cheyne heard the splash and shouted: "That is the end of her." He then came through to Ingram, clapped him on the back, and praised him for being such a good servant. Unknown to Cheyne, the child at that time was being borne over the hills to Dorrery. Lady Cheyne lay grieving for several days, and every time that Reginald came near her, he shouted and swore at her.

Years passed by, and Lady Cheyne bore no more children. The great Cheyne still longed for a son, and at times flew into a passion, and shouted abuse at his wife. At other times, the passion would turn to grief as he thought of his two daughters whom he believed were lying dead at the bottom of the river.

Cheyne had great wealth and power, but when he visited some of his friends' homes, and saw the joy that their young children brought to them, he would sometimes sulk as he thought of the joy he could have derived from his daughters who would now be growing up.

Lady Cheyne often made secret trips to Dorrery to see her two daughters. She always left their nurses with plenty of money to see that they were well provided for. The girls were named Marjory and Mary, and they grew up to be very beautiful. When they were teenagers, their mother made arrangements for them to attend a convent in Murkle, near Thurso, where they were educated.

Reginald Cheyne was now growing old, and the thought that his vast estates would pass to a nephew whom he hardly knew, worried him. When he was alone, the murders of his two daughters weighed heavily on his mind, and began to embitter him. He would see visions of the two tiny babies in shawls at the bottom of the river. At night time he often suffered severe mental anguish as he wrestled with the weight of guilt on his conscience. How he wished that he could turn the clock back so that he could look upon their births with the joy and excitement of a father-to-be. "If only I had forgotten about all my worldly wealth and thought more about the joys of life, I would have been a happier man today," thought Cheyne. "The bible says that unless you become as a little child, you shall not enter into the Kingdom of Heaven, and what is to become of me with the way I have treated my children. I never experienced a father's joy of holding a newborn baby in my arms and looking upon their limbs and wondering about the miracles of birth and creation. No, my joy of power robbed me of this." As time passed, Cheyne's mental anguish grew worse, and from the former defiant, desperate person, it was noticed that he had become a bit quieter. Eventually he began to dread night time, because as he lay in his bed, listening to the sound of the river outside the lodge, his thoughts were with his two baby daughters.

Cheyne still fought to keep his proud, defiant front to the outside world, but inwardly he was becoming a shattered old man. He became more humane in his dealings with his wife and the household servants. He never mentioned his daughters to his wife, but she knew that his conscience was troubling him. As the time was approaching for an annual ball, she secretly made plans to have their daughters, Marjory and Mary, attend the ball.

When the feast was set in the banqueting hall, Cheyne could not take his eyes off two beautiful girls who were seated at the table. Whenever he gazed at them, he thought of his own two daughters who, if they had lived, would be the same age as these two girls. Cheyne tried to put a brave front on things and sound cheerful, but inwardly he was very troubled, with the result that he indulged in more than his fair share of drink. Lady Cheyne was worried by his behaviour and tried to stop him, but he told her to mind her own business.

When the dance started, young men swarmed around the two girls, and they were never off the dance floor. Cheyne could not keep his eyes off them, and inwardly he was fighting a battle with his conscience as he thought of how proud he would have been of his own daughters if they had lived to attend the ball. He tried to console his thoughts with drink, but the more he drank, the more troubled he became, as he thought of how he had arranged for the murder of his infants. At last, he could stand it no longer, so he decided to make a clean breast of the affair. He stood up, threw himself prostrate on the floor, and shouted: "I am a murderer! I am a murderer! I drowned my two daughters!"

The people gathered round him as he lay sobbing on the floor. Lady Cheyne took her two daughters by the hand and led them to where their father lay. Cheyne was overjoyed to see his daughters were still alive and he embraced them. It was some time before he gathered his composure again.

Lady Cheyne then told him how she had conspired with Ingram Gunn to have the babies carried away to Dorrery. She also told how Ingram had exchanged the babies for weighted bundles of clothes which he dropped into the river in their place. Cheyne said: "Up until now I have been a very cruel, greedy man. The more gold I possessed, the more I lusted for. During these last few years, I have learned the value of human love as I longed for my daughters whom I believed were dead. The true love of their mother outwitted my wicked plan, and I thank God for it. Riches never gave me peace of mind as I always wanted to be richer. I believe now that I can have peace of mind so that I can settle with my wife and family, and I ask God to be forgiven for all my past sins."

Bridge over the Thurso River at the end of Loch More which is believed to have been built with stones from Cheyne's hunting lodge

Cheyne showered all the gifts that was possible on his two daughters. He saw to it that their former nurse at Dorrery was well rewarded, and he also looked to the welfare of Ingram Gunn who had deceived him and saved his daughters. Cheyne's attitude to life changed completely, and from a ruthless bully he became a kind, considerate man. He became great friends with his daughters, and his life after that was centred around them.

Marjory fell in love with Nicolaus Sutherland, second son of the Earl of Sutherland. When they married he gifted them Auldwick Castle and lands: Mary married John Keith, second son of Edward Keith, Earl Marischal. She received Ackergill Tower and lands as a wedding gift.

Cheyne was very attached to his lodge at Loch More, and before he died, made a special request that his grave should be filled with sand from Loch More. When Cheyne died he was buried near a chapel at Olrinbeg, Scotscalder, and his grave was filled with sand from his beloved loch.

There are no ruins left of Cheyne's hunting lodge at Loch More. Stones from the last part of the ruins were removed about a hundred years ago and used to build a bridge over Thurso River.

The Beauty of Braemore

IN A LOVELY SECLUDED VALLEY, bordered by the mountains of Scaraben, Maiden Pap, Smean and Morven, lies the hamlet of Braemore, Caithness. The Berriedale River murmurs sweetly as it meanders through the dale on its way to the sea. When the golden rays of the sun fill the valley as it is setting, there is a feeling of peace, perfect peace, and it is difficult to surmise that Braemore at one time experienced very troubled times and bloodshed.

About 1400 Lachlan Gunn was a farmer in Corrichoich, Braemore. His farm house is believed to have been situated on the west side of the Maiden Pap, beside a small stream which is a tributary of the Berriedale River. Lachlan had a daughter, named Helen, who was very beautiful. She had long fair hair and was known as the Beauty of Braemore, and suitors from throughout Caithness often came and tried to seek her hand in marriage, but she declined their offers. From her childhood she had been very friendly with a local boy named Alexander Gunn, and as they grew up, their friendship blossomed into love. They spent their spare time walking around Braemore, and in the sheltered glades, pledged their love for one another.

Dugald Keith of Ackergill, Caithness, who was acting as a factor for some property in Braemore, saw Helen one day while on a visit there, and was immediately captivated by her beauty and charm. At that time the Gunns and the Keiths were on friendly terms. Dugald Keith being a very powerful and proud man immediately called on Lachlan Gunn and told him he would do anything to have his daughter's hand in marriage.

He promised him lands and property on his Ackergill Estate in return for Helen.

"To be wealthy and have plenty of land is what every man dreams of," replied Lachlan, "but to sell my daughter like a cattle beast is something I am not going to do. Helen has been courting Alexander Gunn for a long time and they are to be married shortly."

Dugald Keith tried every means in his power to try and lure Lachlan with offers of gold and other riches in return for Helen's hand, but Lachlan, who was a God-fearing man, would have none of his offers of riches. He considered that his daughter would be happier with Alexander Gunn than with the rich and wicked Keith. Eventually, after all Keith's offers had been refused by Lachlan, he mounted on his horse in a rage and rode away with his party vowing that he would have Helen as his bride in spite of her father's opposition. "Lachlan Gunn will never be able to refuse my offers and live to tell the tale," murmured Keith.

Alexander Gunn was told that Dugald Keith had been infatuated with Helen and had gone to ask her father for her hand in marriage. Alexander immediately became very downcast and worried as he did not think that Lachlan Gunn would refuse Keith's offer of lands and riches in return for his daughter. The thought of having to part with his lovely Helen was more than he could bear to think of. It was a very dejected Alexander who met Helen that night, but when Helen assured him that her father had refused Keith's offer, he was overjoyed and clasped her in his arms. They pledged their undying love for each other and decided to get married.

On the day of the wedding everything went ahead as planned. The guests had assembled in the house and the couple had pledged their vows before the priest. The marriage feast was then served and the company were dancing to the strains of the bagpipes when Dugald Keith barged into the house armed with his broadsword. "I have come to claim my bride!" roared Keith.

"Get out of this house," shouted Lachlan Gunn, "and do not disturb this wedding."

Keith blew a hunting horn and all of a sudden over a hundred Keiths joined him. Very few of the Gunns who were at the wedding were armed, but they armed themselves with pieces of furniture or anything that was available to use as weapons. Though hopelessly outnumbered, the Gunns put up a desperate fight for their lives, and slew several of the invaders before they fell victims to the Keiths' swords. The Keiths killed all the men, but spared the women, Approximately 50 men of the Clan Gunn were killed.

Helen Gunn was kneeling over the body of her husband, sobbing, when she was dragged away by the Keiths. Dugald Keith surveyed the macabre scene with a look of triumph in his eyes, and ordered Helen to be strapped to a horse.

Wailing and sobbing, Helen, in her white bridal dress, with her hands bound behind her back, was strapped on to a horse. The hills around Braemore have seen many sad scenes, but this must have been the most tragic ever, as Helen, screaming and wailing, was borne away from her home while the other women of the district were wailing over the bodies of their dead husbands. The scene of sorrow in Braemore that day defies any description.

Helen cried all the way to Dunbeath Castle, where Dugald Keith intended to spend the night with Sutherland of Dunbeath. She was carried into a room where she was placed under a strong guard. Dugald Keith drank bumpers of strong ale as he told Sutherland how he had killed all the Gunns at the wedding in Braemore. "All the men of Braemore are dead," said Dugald, "and only ten of my men were killed."

"You have cleared Braemore of all the vermin," said Sutherland, who was continually having skirmishes with the Gunns.

"Long live the Sutherlands and the Keiths and death to the Gunns," said Dugald, as he raised his glass in salute.

When the drink had taken effect on Dugald Keith, he decided to pay a visit to Helen Gunn. By this time Helen was lying quiet in her room, in her torn wedding dress, and her tears had run dry. She was exhausted with sobbing. Keith approached her in jovial mood, and tried to sympathise with her for the death of her husband.

"Get out! You base murderer!" she shouted, and kicked him in the shins.

Dugald Keith flew into a temper, and shouted: "You vile bitch! I will learn you not to treat a respectable member of the clan Keith like this," and he kicked her several times as she lay on the floor before he left her room. In a bitter temper Keith went to his bed in Dunbeath Castle that night.

The next morning he reassembled his party and ordered them to march to Ackergill Castle with Helen Gunn as their prisoner. She was imprisoned in a bedroom on one of the top floors of the castle and a strong guard was left to watch over her in case she tried to escape.

Dugald Keith often went into her room and tried to get on friendly terms with her by asking her to become his lady. She refused to have anything to do with him, and called him a dirty dog and the vile murderer of her husband. Keith could never stand to be called a murderer and always flew into a rage and beat Helen until she was unconscious.

Helen was kept a prisoner for more than two months, but ill-treatment and continual beatings by Dugald Keith failed to break her courageous spirit, and she took every opportunity that she could find to let him know how much she loathed him and his clan. The effects of imprisonment and the murder of her husband, however, changed her countenance. From being the Beauty of Braemore with long fair hair, she now looked like an old woman as her locks had turned to grey.

Dugald Keith kept up his visits to her room, but she always rejected his advances, and he always ill-treated her before he left the room. Keith then roamed around the castle having rows with members of the staff. The cause of his vile temper was that he was finding it impossible to break the spirit of Helen Gunn.

One day Helen sat in her room praying for her mother, young brothers and sisters in Braemore. Horror struck her as she thought of her Alexander, her father, and the other men from Braemore who had been murdered at the wedding. Her day of joy had become one of terrible sorrow. She also thought of Keith's offer to make her the Lady of Ackergill if she would accept him as her husband. "My heart has always been with Alexander, and with him it will remain until I die. I could never replace the love in my heart for Alexander and my father with money and riches. To think that I could spend the rest of my life with their murderer sickens me to death. My life has always been pure and it will be pure to the end. That black-hearted Keith shall never have me,

I shall be happier in heaven with Alexander than I shall ever be in this place. Dugald Keith showed no mercy towards the men of Braemore, and he shall show no mercy towards me." She listened to the sound of the wind and the waves outside the castle, and thought how much happier she would be with Alexander in the promised land than a prisoner in Ackergill Castle. Helen's guards had left the room for a short time, and she thought: "this is the time to join my love." A vision of Alexander appeared in front of her so she broke a pane of glass in the window, climbed out on the ledge, and with a prayer to commend her spirit to God, she jumped towards the ground, far below.

The guards heard the sound of breaking glass and rushed into the room to find that Helen was missing. They looked out of the window and saw her broken body lying on the ground. Several of the servants also heard the sound of breaking glass and rushed out of the castle to find Helen's dead body.

The servants were all dumbfounded at what had happened. They were all afraid of their bullying laird, Dugald Keith, but had great admiration for the fight Helen had put up against him. A terrible sense of sorrow gripped them and they all stood round in complete silence, and many were in tears. Finally the silence was broken by an old man who said: "Today we have witnessed a terrible deed in the history of Clan Keith. As we stand here, we gaze on the feeble, broken body of a young girl, but what a girl! Her courage has shown us there is a difference between right and wrong. Our Laird has always believed that he can have everything he wants because of his money and power, but Helen showed he could not have her. I have always believed that love is the most beautiful thing in the world, and Helen has clearly showed us this. When she made her marriage vows in Braemore, she had no intention of breaking them, or being lured away from her husband by money and riches. Our Laird killed her husband and the men of Braemore, but he was never able to kill the love for her husband which burned in her breast. She has shown us that love is the most powerful weapon in the world when it overcame even Dugald Keith's sword. The name of our Laird will go down in history as a blackguard and a murderer, but the name of Helen Gunn will live on as a symbol of love, truth and fidelity."

Ackergill Castle, where Helen jumped to her death

The servants were very impressed by the brave words spoken by the man and when they were able to gather their composure, they carried Helen's body to a field on the west side of the castle where they buried her near the beach. A flat stone was placed over the grave with the name Helen Gunn inscribed on it. This stone was visible about fifty years ago, but it has now disappeared and it is believed that it may be buried in the sandy soil or it may have been removed by the military during the Second World War when they were building fortifications in the area.

A flagstone, measuring five feet eight inches in height by three feet in breadth, has been used to close a door of a shed in the field on the west side of the castle. The stone is covered with moss and the imprint of the body of a woman can be seen among the moss. The impression measures approximately five feet in height. Local tradition states that this flagstone at one time formed part of the pavement in front of Ackergill Castle and that it was the stone on which Helen landed when she jumped to her death. It is very old and is about one and a half inches thick. Whatever is the explanation for the phenomenon of the impression of the woman's body, we do not know, but it appears to be a memorial to some dastardly deed which took place in Ackergill Castle.

Many poems were written to commemorate the courage of Helen of Braemore. James Traill Calder describes the attack on their house in one of the stanzas of his poem:

> *The clash of swords and the shouts of men arise,*
> *Mingled with women's heart-rending cries,*
> *The gallant Gunns, tho' they fought nobly all,*
> *But in the end, overpowered and butchered fall,*
> *Among the rest, the bridegroom on the floor,*
> *Pierced deep with his wounds, lies weltering in his gore,*
> *But who may paint the anguish of his bride?*
> *Ah! happier far, if she too had died?*
> *In frantic agony she tore her hair,*
> *That fell dishevelled round her forehead fair,*
> *And prayed to heaven to avenge the deed of blood,*
> *And smite the ruthless murderers where they stood,*
> *In vain she wept - in vain to heaven did pray -*
> *Distracted, screaming, she is borne away*
> *By the fell hands that laid her husband low,*
> *To drink on earth the bitterest cup of woe.*

The tragic death of Helen Gunn started a bitter feud between Clan Gunn and the Clan Keith which lasted for several hundreds of years. In 1978 both clans decided that it was time to end this feud, so on 28th July 1978, at a gathering of the Clan Gunn in Caithness, a charter of friendship was signed by the Commander of Clan Gunn and the Chief of Clan Keith.

The words of the old man have now come true, and although more than five hundred years have passed since the death of Helen Gunn, Dugald Keith is remembered as a ruthless murderer, while Helen is remembered as a symbol of beauty and true love.

The Prisoner's Leap

THE DUNBEATH RIVER, IN CAITHNESS, flows through the Dunbeath Strath at the end of its course to the sea. This was once the scene of a thriving community, but is now desolate, due to the evictions of the nineteenth century. At Crageneath the river is guarded on both sides by perpendicular rock faces. The rock on the north side of the gorge is approximately one hundred feet in height, while that on the south side is about seventy feet, and the distance is approximately thirty-five feet between the two. This gorge is known as the Prisoner's Leap, and tradition tells us that it was jumped by a man in the sixteenth century. It happened this way...

A daughter of one of the Clan Gunn in Braemore gave birth to an illegitimate male child, and she died shortly after the birth. Her mother and father took care of the child and, as it was approaching winter, there was no cow's milk available, they fed him on milk from a tame hind. The child was named Ian McMormack Gunn, and to distinguish him from other members of the clan, he was known as Ian McMormack. He thrived well on the hind's milk, and it soon became evident to his grandparents that he possessed tremendous strength.

When Ian was just over one year old his grandmother took him to the hill while she was working at the peats. She set him down in the heather near the peat bank, so that she could watch him. It was a very hot summer's day and Ian gurgled with joy as he pulled out handfuls of heather. Suddenly, his grandmother heard a hissing sound and looked around in horror to see a large adder making straight for the child. Before

View of Braemore

she could reach Ian, he stretched out his hand, grasped the snake around the neck, and was shaking it backwards and forwards, still making happy gurgling sounds. When she was able to make Ian release the snake, it lay lifeless in the heather, strangled by the power of his grip.

Ian grew up to be very strong and muscular, and this was believed to be due to his early feeding. When he was eight years old he could out-run and out-jump boys twice his age. His grandparents took great pride in his feats of strength, and this was said to be consolation for the disgrace that their late daughter had caused by having an illegitimate child. At that time, to have a child outwith wedlock was one of the worst sins to be committed. Some people believed that Ian McMormack had been sent by God to Braemore to act as a divine protector of the Clan Gunn against their many enemies. One old woman said, "Moses was sent to lead the children of Israel to the promised land, and Ian McMormack was sent to Braemore to protect and guide the Clan Gunn."

When Ian McMormack grew to manhood, he was so strong that he could fell an ox with one blow, and so swift of foot that he could outrun a horse at full gallop. He was made personal bodyguard to the chief of Clan Gunn, and accompanied him on all his forays against the Keiths and Sinclairs. Sometimes on these forays he would be armed with a sword, sometimes with a club but, whatever his weapon, it always made tremendous slaughter against the enemy. When using a sword, his agility was such that his opponent could not see the blade, it moved so swiftly. Armed with a club, he smashed both the swords and the skulls of his unfortunate opponents.

Enemies of the Gunns were so afraid of him that for a long time they lived at peace with them. But the Sinclairs and the Keiths were jealous of the reputation Ian was setting throughout the north and they fell to wondering how they might destroy him.

The Keiths, who lived in Forse Castle, had their own champion, Angus Mor MacKay, a native of Strathnaver. He had been in the service of their chief for several years, but was not believed to be a match for Ian McMormack. On two or three occasions he had almost come face to face with Ian McMormack in battles with the Gunns, but before he actually encountered the renowned warrior his courage failed and he fled at the sight of the slaughter being inflicted by Ian. Angus Mor thought it was better to run and live than stand and die.

When not engaged in battle, Ian was a very peaceful and gentle man. His strength was always at the service of the weak and the aged, and he was a great favourite with young children. He was so quiet in his manner that it was hard to believe he was such a terror in battle. Ian also was a deeply religious man and believed that each victory that he won was the work of a higher authority. After every battle he spent a long time in prayer.

Ian's great strength must place him among the great strong men of all time, but his particular talent was his tremendous speed. His reflexes were so fast that he could catch a fly in his hand and then release it without causing it any injury. He could wield a broadsword or a club with such speed that it was not visible to the human eye. It was a special gift which won him the name: 'The Human Tornado of the Clan Gunn', and gave him supremacy over all other men.

Ian loved the spring of the heather under his feet and the fresh wind in his face, and he spent long hours hunting on the hill. He could race down and catch a stag and then kill it with a blow of his fist. No other hunter in Caithness was ever able to employ the same method. While the Clan Gunn was living in peace with his neighbours, Ian spent most of his time hunting in the hills. He knew every crag and corrie around the Braemore, Dunbeath and Latheron districts.

On hot sunny days he often lay down in the hills to have a sleep after a long walk in the heather. News of this habit reached the Chief of the Keiths, so he sent a scout to watch McMormack. The scout reported back to the chief that nearly every day McMormack went for a walk in the hills around Braemore, and often lay down in the heather and slept.

The chief rubbed his hands together with glee: "At last, I am going to capture big Ian McMormack, who has defeated my people in every fight that we have had with the Gunns. I intend to consult my friend Sinclair, Laird of Dunbeath, and have a strong party of Keiths with my henchman, Angus Mor MacKay, sent to Dunbeath Strath, so that they can be concealed there by the Sinclairs. When the opportunity arises, they can capture Ian McMormack when he is fast asleep. I will hang him by the neck in the forecourt of the castle and then wreak vengeance on the Gunns. I cannot wait until I see Angus Mor's sword cutting the Gunns to pieces without Ian McMormack to stop him. Great will be the slaughter and all the glory will go to the Keiths."

Keith rode to Dunbeath Castle where he had a conference with Sinclair. Their interests were mutual, and Sinclair agreed to give Keith every assistance in his attempt to capture Ian McMormack. Returning to Forse Castle, the Chief of the Keiths picked forty of his best men and put them under the leadership of Angus Mor MacKay. Under cover of darkness they marched to Dunbeath Strath, where they hid in the homes of Sinclair tenants.

The next day, scouts were sent into the hills around Braemore to keep watch for Ian McMormack. About noon he was seen walking up Achinavish Hill, wearing only his kilt, as the sun was so hot. He walked on until he came to the Wag Hill, and then lay down in the heather to sleep.

The scout immediately went to Dunbeath Strath and informed Angus Mor MacKay. The raiding party were quickly assembled and they went to the Wag Hill where Ian McMormack lay sleeping. Angus Mor and the party cautiously approached him, and when they were a few feet away, they sprang upon him. Ian awoke and put up a desperate fight for his life, but the odds were so overwhelming that he was overpowered and bound hand and foot. He was then strapped to a horse and taken to Forse Castle.

The Chief of the Keiths was overwhelmed with joy when he saw Angus Mor and his party return to the castle with McMormack their prisoner. He immediately sent for his advisers and Sinclair of Dunbeath to decide the best way to dispose of him. Keith was adamant that they should immediately hang him in the forecourt of the castle, but some of his advisers were against him coming to any quick decision. Sinclair agreed with Keith that he should be hanged immediately, but one of his advisers asked: "On what crime can we sentence McMormack to death?"

"Murder!" replied Keith. "He slew fifty of my best men in our last battle with the Gunns."

"It is not murder to kill a man in battle," replied the adviser. "I have lived in Dunbeath Strath all of my life and Ian McMormack has never hurt a hair on any person's head other than when he has been attacked or engaged in battle. His feats are legends around the Highlands of Caithness, where he is the protector of the weak and oppressed. His good deeds are not only confined to his own clan. Only the other day I saw him carry home peats for an old widow Sinclair in Dunbeath Strath. The Borders of Caithness and Sutherland will erupt if any harm falls on McMormack, and I doubt if Forse Castle will last more than a few hours against their vengeance. McMormack is probably the greatest athlete that ever lived and, like Samson, great will be the slaughter at his death. I fully believe that McMormack is given his power from above, and I advise that we deal mercifully with him."

"Nonsense!" shouted Keith. "Call out the hangman and let us see him dangling from a rope."

Sinclair interrupted quietly: "There is something in what my servant has said. I think we should consider matters carefully before we come to any decision on McMormack. A number of my people in Dunbeath Strath have a great respect for him. If the Gunns of Braemore, Gunns of Kildonan and Gunns of Dirlot joined with the clan Sutherland and some of my own people, I doubt if we would survive very long against them. We must try to kill McMormack in some cunning way and make it look as if his death was not really intended."

"The surest way to kill a man is to string him from the end of a rope. Let us do that and stop wasting time," said Keith. "We are only giving the Clan Gunn a chance to muster when they find that McMormack is missing. Order the hangman to get the gallows ready and we shall have the pleasure of seeing him hanging in a short time."

"Listen to my plan!" said Sinclair. "Ian McMormack Gunn is said to be one of the greatest athletes of all time. I know that he is good, but I also know that you have a great athlete in Angus Mor MacKay. MacKay is really no match for McMormack, but he will fit in very well with my plan. On the Dunbeath River there is the Crageneath Gorge, which is very high and wide, and I know that it would be impossible for any man to jump across it. We could arrange for Ian McMormack and Angus to run a race to Dunbeath Strath, and if Ian McMormack could jump across the gorge, he would be set free. I know that it is impossible for any person to jump across the gorge and he would be smashed to pieces on the rocks below. We then would be rid of our greatest enemy, and yet people would not accuse us of killing him."

"Sinclair, you are very cunning and wise," said Keith. "Tomorrow we shall all ride to Crageneath and see McMormack smashed to pieces on the rocks. We shall leave this Castle early and be in position before noon, because at that time I want Ian McMormack and Angus Mor to begin their race. Guards must be placed all along the route and on all parts of Dunbeath River to make sure that McMormack does not escape. We shall drink a bumper of ale when McMormack dies and then we shall leave his body on the rocks so that the ravens can pick his bones. Tomorrow will be a great day for the Keiths and the Sinclairs."

The night was then spent in feasting and dancing at Forse Castle to celebrate the forthcoming death of Ian McMormack.

During the night it rained and by next morning the Dunbeath River was in spate. In the early morning Keith's retainers and Sinclair's took up their positions all along the route of the intended race and on the north bank of the Dunbeath River. They were all armed with broadswords and the only place left unguarded was the gorge. Before noon Keith and Sinclair and their party rode into a position just west of the gorge where they had a grandstand view. Here there waited a very macabre party – expecting to see the jump to death.

Ian McMormack lay in the dungeon of Forse Castle. He felt that he did not have long to live before the Keiths would hang him, so he spent the time in prayer.

He prayed for help and protection for his grandparents in Braemore after he was dead. "They have been proud of me all their lives and would be proud if they were here to see me die. I have faced all the troubles and trials of life in a cheerful manner and shall meet death cheerfully. I shall walk on the scaffold as if I were going for a walk on Morven and I will show the Keiths that even death cannot conquer the spirit of Ian McMormack."

The gate of the dungeon was then opened and Ian prepared himself for his fate. He was led to the forecourt of the castle where he expected to see a gallows ready, but to his surprise there stood Angus Mor. One of the Keiths called: "Our Chief has decided to show mercy unto you. If you beat our champion, Angus Mor MacKay, in a race and then jump across the gorge on Dunbeath River at Crageneath, you will have gained your freedom."

The ruins of Forse Castle

Prisoner's Leap, Dunbeath Strath

The irons were then removed from Ian McMormack, and at a signal from one of the Keiths, the race began. Angus Mor rushed off at a swift pace, leaving Ian McMormack behind, for he was stiff and sore after being in irons. They had barely covered half a mile when the blood began to circulate again in Ian's veins, and he overtook Angus Mor. With a flying leap, he crossed the Latheron Burn, and raced towards the Latheronwheel Burn, which he crossed in the same manner. Climbing up towards the higher ground which separates Latheronwheel from Dunbeath, his pace began to slacken, and Angus Mor was gaining ground on him. Ian was thinking deeply. There were Sinclair and Keith guards all along the route and he could think of no way of escape. The gorge was very wide. Could he jump it?

His pace was reasonably slow as he was approaching the Houstry Burn, Dunbeath, but by this time his mind was finally made up. He was either going to jump the gorge, or die in the attempt. He cantered towards the Houstry Burn, jumped it, and then stopped. Angus Mor raced past him and thought Ian McMormack had given up, but Ian stood, looked around for a few seconds, as if gathering up all his resources, and then set off at a fast pace. He passed Angus Mor at such a speed that it looked as if Angus was walking. Ian thundered towards the Learanaich Burn, which he cleared in his stride, and raced on towards higher ground approaching Crageneath Gorge.

Angus Mor was a long way behind as Ian sped on as if possessed by a demon. He raced towards the edge of the precipice and, with one bound, soared upwards like an eagle. His kilt seemed to act as wings as he drifted towards the other side, but he landed a few feet short of the rock. However, as he fell, he grasped a tree at the top of the rock, and pulled himself to safety.

Keiths' and Sinclairs' parties fired a hail of arrows at him, but he was able to evade them as he made his way towards Braemore and safety. The Keiths and Sinclairs returned to their homes that night, knowing that once again Ian McMormack had cheated death.

McMormack is reputed to have lived to an old age and died in his bed, but the story of his great feat lives on. The distance between the rocks at Crageneath at the time when Ian McMormack jumped it was said to be more than fifty feet. Whether this is true or not we do not know, as the distance between rocks can alter with the passage of time.

The Giant of Morven

STORIES OF MYSTERY AND IMAGINATION have thrilled men from earliest times. No story is more thrilling or mysterious than that which surrounds the Black Bodach, or the giant of Morven. The hamlet of Braemore in Caithness is now very sparsely populated, but in olden times, it was very different. The main livelihood for the villagers has always been crofting. Winter sometimes comes early in Braemore, and when this happens, the oats fail to ripen, and the crop is lost. After the onset of an early winter, the inhabitants would spend their savings to buy oats which were then ground into meal at the local mill. The people always had to work hard in order to wrest a meagre living from the soil, and they despised any person who would not work.

One autumn, when winter had come early to Braemore and the crops had failed, a dark-haired man appeared in the district. No one knew where he had come from. Rumours that he was an agent from the nether regions began to creep round the district. He was always begging for food from the people, and although they had little to eat themselves, they were charitable folk. The stranger wandered round the district, sleeping in barns, but never doing any work. After some time, the people grew tired of providing food for him. A meeting was held in one of the elder's houses, and it was resolved that any more requests for food from the stranger would be refused.

On the next day, the dark-haired stranger called at one of the houses in the district, and asked for food. His request was refused, so he called at all the other houses where he received the same answer. He then flew into a violent temper and shouted, "If I am going to get nothing to eat, you folk will have little pleasure in your eating." He then walked towards the meal mill, hoisted the upper millstone on to his back and walked off towards Morven. By removing the millstone he had rendered the mill useless and the miller was unable to grind any more meal.

The stranger was not seen in Braemore again, but shortly afterwards, sheep and cattle began to disappear. A watch on the houses and animals was kept, but the robber was not seen.

Some of the wise women of the district were consulted, but they were unable to say who was responsible for the thefts. The replies given by some of the women seemed to indicate that perhaps it was the local men who were responsible. The men of the district were furious that suspicion should be cast upon them, and a meeting was called in the house of the chief elder of Braemore. The meeting began with prayer, and after the elder had deliberated for some time, he said that the robber was a disciple of the Devil, and was empowered to make himself invisible to ordinary human eyes. The elder believed that the best way to combat this evil power was to continue the watch over the cattle on the hill to see what would happen.

Morven

A few days later, the men were keeping watch on the hills near Morven, when they saw the stranger striding through the hills. He had now assumed gigantic proportions, and was carrying a huge bow in his hands. He stalked along the hills, through a herd of cattle, shot the best bullock with an arrow, hoisted the carcase to his shoulders, and strode off towards Morven. The men emerged from their hiding places, but the stranger, or Black Bodach, bounded off towards Morven just as a heavy mist came down suddenly over the hill, shrouding the giant from sight.

The men searched around the hillside in the mist, but could find no trace of the robber. They waited on Morven until the mist cleared, but they could still see no sign of him, so they had to return to Braemore and tell their tale.

A council was held, and it was resolved that the watch should be kept up, and that the watchers be supplied with as much food and drink as required until the Black Bodach was captured. The watchers, who were happy in the thought that they would become heroes if they captured the Black Bodach, kept a diligent vigil in the hills. Robberies from the houses continued, but at no time was any person seen at any of the places where jewellery and other valuable goods were stolen.

On several occasions the Black Bodach was sighted stalking herds of cattle on the hill and killing the best beast in the herd. He then slung it over his shoulders and ran away towards Morven. The watchers always pursued him, but every time a thick mist would engulf the mountain, and the Black Bodach disappeared in it. The men became disheartened with the failure of their efforts, and rumours began to circulate that their lack of success was due to the barley beer in which they were indulging.

After having kept watch for several weeks, the men decided that they would have to find some other means of capturing or killing the elusive robber. One of the wise women of Braemore was again consulted. She was very reluctant to discuss the strange events that were taking place, but eventually told them to consult a witch who lived near Braemore. The witch was approached, and she, too, was reluctant to discuss the matter. The men accused her of being a disciple of the Devil, and they threatened that if she would not help them they would burn her at the stake as a witch. She then relented and said that there was a woman living in Sutherland who could help them. This woman had a brother who lived on Morven who might be the Bodach.

The men went to Sutherland and found the woman. She denied that she was any relation of the Black Bodach, but refused to help them. They then accused her also of being a witch, and again threatened her with being burned to death if she would not help them. She then admitted she was a sister of the Black Bodach. They asked her how they could break his power over the mist on Morven. She told them that they must keep watch for him on the seventh day of the seventh month, because on that particular day he had no power over the mist. The men returned to their homes in Braemore and waited for the seventh of July.

On the night of the sixth of July the men armed themselves with swords, bows and arrows, and took up position near Morven. Early next morning the Black Bodach appeared and began to stalk a herd of cattle. The men emerged from their places of concealment and gave chase. The Black Bodach ran away towards Morven, and this time the mist did not come down to cover his escape. He ran towards his den, shouting strange words in Gaelic in an attempt to bring the mist down, and he disappeared from view into a hole in the hillside. When his pursuers came near it they could hear him still muttering magic words in an attempt to bring down the mist.

The Black Bodach placed the missing millstone over the entrance to his den and then began to fire arrows through the hole at his pursuers. Dodging the arrows, the men of Braemore approached the den. They were just about to rush forward to storm it when the Bodach threw aside the millstone and came out. He seemed to be suddenly stricken with lameness, for he limped as he ran away over the mountain.

The searchers looked into his den, and the sight which greeted their eyes put Aladdin's Cave to shame – it was stacked with gold, jewels, and other ornaments. After sticking an arrow in the ground to mark the den, they gave chase, but by this time the Black Bodach had travelled a considerable distance and it was some time before they were able to catch up with him. They fired arrows at him, but the arrows just glanced off his body. Earlier, several ropes had been laid in the heather in an attempt to trip the Bodach, and eventually he tripped on one of them and fell. The pursuers set upon him and bound him hand and foot with their ropes.

When the Black Bodach saw that he was overpowered by the men of Braemore, he began to plead for mercy and promised that he would never trouble them again if they would spare his life. But the men paid little attention to his pleas.

"Let us burn him on the spot and then we can share out his treasure among us," said one of them.

"Take my treasure, but spare my life," said Bodach, "if you kill me you shall never get my treasure."

"Nonsense!" shouted the men. "How can he take his treasure from us after he is dead?"

"The treasure belongs to me and the mountain, and no person shall get it without my consent," said the Bodach, "I have taken away cattle, food and riches from you, but I have never killed anyone. Life is the greatest treasure in the world, and he that taketh away life shall never be rich. The hills and the mountains provide food for you, and in return I have been taking some of your treasures. The hills and I must be repaid in some way," he finished.

But the men's heads were filled with nothing but thoughts of riches, and they paid no attention to the Bodach's pleadings. They quickly built a pyre of heather, and when it was burning fiercely, they threw the Bodach into the heart of it. His cries as the fire consumed him rocked the mountain like thunder.

When the body of the Bodach was reduced to cinders, the men decided to go and share out the treasure, but when they reached the spot where they thought the millstone was marked by an arrow, they found not one arrow, but several hundred arrows marking different spots, and no trace at all of the millstone or the Bodach's den. They searched until nightfall, still without success. The next day all the inhabitants of Braemore went to Morven and searched, but they, too, were unable to find the buried stone, or the buried treasure.

Climbers on Morven, who had never heard the legend, have told how they saw a large millstone on the mountain. They then tried to guide the local people up to it, but were unable to find it again. It is said that the millstone is never seen more than once by any person. The last reported sighting was about eighty years ago.

Morven still retains the mystery of the giant and the treasure. Arguments have raged for years as to whether the Black Bodach was an omen of good or evil, and as opinions may differ, this has never been settled. When thunder rumbles over Morven, it is sometimes said to be the voice of the Black Bodach, warning the people to keep away from the treasure. The story of the Black Bodach has lived for a long time, and the mystery of it deepens as the years go by.

Graysteel -
the Robber of Loch Rangag

IN AN ENCHANTED SETTING AMONG the hills of Rangag, Latheron, Caithness, beside where the Causewaymire Road winds its way through the moors to Georgemas, lies beautiful Loch Rangag. This small loch is sheltered on the east by the hill of Stemster, and on the west by Coire na Beine; away to the south-west tower the ramparts of the mountains of Scaraben and Morven, as if guarding Caithness from the county of Sutherland.

It seems hard to believe that a few hundred years ago this delightful spot was a forbidden land, and any person who ventured here was lucky to escape with his life. On a small peninsula by the side of the loch is a small mound of stones – the ruins of a small castle or keep. The ruin is now out on a peninsula, but it appears that at one time it must have been surrounded by water. In this castle in the early seventeenth century lived a notorious robber and freebooter by the name of Graysteel. His dates are in doubt, though some believe that he lived about the thirteenth century, and from the information available it appears that it was around the late sixteenth and early seventeenth centuries.

Graysteel (his real name is not known) was a man of powerful build and great strength. He was an expert swordsman and no person who ever encountered him in a conflict ever lived to tell the tale. Some folk believed him to be a disciple of the Devil, set up by his master in the castle of Loch Rangag to wreak vengeance on the people of Caithness for their religious views.

Many tales of kindness are told of Rob Roy and other robbers, but no such compassion seemed to exist in Graysteel's make-up. He showed no respect for human life and had a lust for inflicting cruelty on people. It was often said that in his sword fights, he would stop fighting when he knew that an opponent was mortally wounded, so that he could watch him die a slow and painful death. Graysteel's cruelty seemed to have such an hypnotic effect on the residents of the county that any requests by him for money or goods was immediately complied with. Folk believed that it was better to stay alive in poverty than to be killed by the sword of the evil one.

Graysteel and his companions often made raids into the adjoining county of Sutherland where they carried off large numbers of cattle and other treasures. On several of these raids he was surprised by the natives, but always his expert swordsmanship turned the odds in his favour.

Another of his favourite hunting grounds was the Ord of Caithness, where he would rob travellers going to and from Caithness. At that time, the road across the Ord lay along the top of the cliffs above the sea. Graysteel used to waylay travellers where the road was narrowest above the precipice. After relieving them of their money and their possessions, he would throw them over the precipice into the sea. The cries of the unfortunate traveller would be heard above the roar of the waves, mingling with the loud, mocking laughter of Graysteel.

When Graysteel was in residence in his castle by Loch Rangag, he boasted that no person ever set foot on his land and lived. Everyone whom he saw trespassing on his land he killed with his sword. One day, while hunting in the Latheron area, a young son of Sinclair of Rattar accidentally strayed onto Graysteel's land. Word was brought to Graysteel that a man was hunting at the west end of the loch, and he immediately set out with his sword and shield. Young Sinclair was a mere youth, and no match for the skill and physique of Graysteel, but the thought that it was an uneven match never entered Graysteel's head as he advanced towards Sinclair and bellowed his challenge.

Sinclair at once drew his sword to defend himself. Being a young man of high spirits, he managed to fight back for a short time with great dexterity until at last he received a mortal blow. As was his custom,

Graysteel threw the body into the loch after he had stripped it of all its valuables. He then strode back to his castle, gloating that he had disposed of another intruder. Little did he know the consequences that were to follow the death of young Sinclair of Rattar.

When the news of the death of their son reached the Rattar family, it plunged them into deep distress and mourning. His young sister, sixteen years of age and a maiden of great beauty, took the news worst of all, and fell into fits of sobbing for several days. Her parents began to fear that she was going to succumb to a broken heart. She had just been engaged to be married to young Sinclair, the Laird of Dunn, Watten, a bosom friend of her late brother.

On hearing the news, Dunn saddled one of his horses and rode to Rattar where he found his betrothed in an almost unconscious state of grief. Dunn stayed with her for two or three days, until she was stronger. Then, before he left, Dunn went to her father and told him that he intended to go to Loch Rangag and challenge Graysteel to a duel, so that he could avenge the death of his friend.

"You must be mad!" exclaimed her father. "There is no swordsman in Scotland who would last more than a few minutes against Graysteel. Go home in peace and forget about avenging the death of my son. The good Lord in his own time will pay back Graysteel for all the atrocities he has committed. Remember that the mills of God work slow but sure."

Dunn did not argue with the Laird of Rattar. He went to bid farewell to his betrothed, and after expressing his love for her in the tenderest terms, made her a solemn vow that he would avenge the death of her brother.

She begged him not to be so foolish. "The body of my brother lies in Loch Rangag, and if your body was to join him there I would surely die of a broken heart. No power on earth can deal with the evil powers of Graysteel."

"The powers of evil must be destroyed," declared Dunn, "and with the help of God I will destroy Graysteel. When I have done that, you will become my Lady Dunn."

So confident did Dunn sound that eventually Miss Sinclair agreed that he should tackle Graysteel, and he departed from Rattar with her blessing and a prayer. She also promised that she would mention his plans to no one.

The Laird returned to Dunn and told some of his retainers of his plan to challenge Graysteel. They warned him that such a plan would be futile since Graysteel was one of the best swordsmen who ever lived.

Dunn then went to the home of one of his chief advisers, an old soldier who lived in a croft on the Hill of Dunn. He told the old man what he intended to do.

"No, my good friend!" said the old man. "I have heard it said that Graysteel can engage ten men at once in combat and beat the lot. To tackle Graysteel single-handed would be to throw your life away. The only way you can destroy Graysteel would be to approach his castle at night when he is asleep and set it on fire."

This treacherous way of dealing with Graysteel did not impress the young Laird, and he returned to his home distressed that no person would agree with his plans. He retired to bed very unhappy, wondering how he would return to his fiancée again if he did not destroy Graysteel. The more he thought about it, the more it troubled him. He tossed about in bed, unable to get any peace of mind, and eventually rose, dressed, and went for a walk.

It was a beautiful moonlit night as he wandered slowly towards the west shores of Loch Watten, where the moonbeams were shimmering across the peaceful waters of the loch. He thought to himself that at least these waters are peaceful on a night like this and the waters of Loch Rangag must be the same. But I can no longer find peace of mind or body until I challenge Graysteel to a duel; I shall either succeed or lie dead at the bottom of Loch Rangag. His mind was made up and he returned to the castle, went to bed and slept soundly until morning.

When Dunn arose, he went about his work as if there was nothing on his mind. His retainers decided that their master had decided to abandon his plan to deal with Graysteel. Then, later in the day, he quietly equipped himself with his best sword and shield, and slipped out of the castle on foot unnoticed. He intended to spend the night in the hills near Loch Rangag and in the morning issue his challenge to Graysteel.

As he left Dunn, black clouds were gathering in the sky and he had not travelled very far across the moors when all the fury of the heavens was unleashed on him. The wind rose to gale force, dashing rain with vehement force into his face. Flashes of lightning and peals of thunder added terror to the storm. Dunn looked round for a place to shelter. A few yards ahead, he saw a lighted cottage window. He knocked, and the door was opened by an old widow who invited him in. Though bent with age and infirmities, her face seemed to radiate some special quality, and Dunn noticed as he entered that a Bible was lying open on a stool beside the fire.

"It is little indeed" she said, "that I have to offer, but He who tendeth the young ravens in the wilderness has never allowed me to want." She made oatmeal brose for Dunn, which he thoroughly enjoyed.

Suddenly, Dunn noticed in one corner a very unusual-looking sword. He was greatly struck by its appearance. The hilt was covered over with a variety of jewels and strange carvings, which seemed to indicate that it was of foreign origin. His curiosity was so much aroused that he asked the old woman how she came by it.

"That sword was the property of my late husband, William MacKay, a sergeant in Lord Reay's regiment. He went with them to Germany and was for some time in the service of Gustavus Adolphus, King of Sweden. I have often heard my husband speak of the way he came by it. It happened when the regiment was lying in some town – I think it was called Frankfurt-on-the-Oder. One day William came upon a set of ruffians ill-treating a Polish Jew. My husband was shocked at their cruelty and, being strong as well as brave, he rushed to his assistance, beat off the attackers and rescued him."

"The poor Jew was so grateful to my husband for saving his life that he made him a present of his sword, which he said he got in Palestine. He assured him that the weapon was endowed with wonderful properties, and that as long as he wielded it, he could never be overcome. After the battle of Lutzen, my husband retired from the service and retired to his native country, bringing the sword with him. He had frequently been offered large sums of money for it, but he never could be induced to dispose of it. On his death-bed he made me promise not to part with it on any consideration; but to keep it as a memorial to himself, and an heirloom for the family. Amidst all my poverty I have religiously adhered to his dying wish, and while I still breathe, it shall never be the property of another."

Dunn then told her who he was, and that he was on his way to Loch Rangag to kill Graysteel, who had treacherously killed his friend. He asked the widow if she would lend him the sword for one day, so that he could use its special properties against Graysteel.

She replied, "Graysteel is an evil man who possesses the power of the Devil. If I were to lend you this sword, it would fall into his possession, since he would surely slay you. Graysteel has lived for a long time in the castle on Loch Rangag, and no man has stood up to his swordsmanship for more than a few minutes. You are a decent young man and, if you value your life, go home and forget Graysteel."

But Dunn said, "Your husband in his lifetime fought against the powers of evil. Graysteel is an agent of the Devil, and a menace to the county. No honest person in this county can go about his business in peace without the fear of Graysteel and his followers. I feel that I have been given a divine order to destroy him. Please give me the loan of your husband's sword for one day so that I can accomplish my task!"

He pleaded with her until at last the widow relented and said he could have a loan of the sword for one day only. After kneeling in prayer on the floor of the cottage, they both retired for the night and slept soundly until first light. The storm abated during the night, and by morning the wind and rain had ceased. The widow gave Dunn breakfast, they then knelt together on the floor in prayer and the widow prayed that Dunn would be given the strength for the task ahead of him. After a final blessing on the sword from the widow, Dunn strapped it round his waist. He then bade her good-bye and set out for Graysteel's castle.

The widow's house was at Halsary and Dunn made his way over the moors in a southerly direction towards Rangag. A lark sang blithely overhead while a bright morning sun was dispersing the mists that shrouded the tops of the hills. Dunn had a feeling of great peace and confidence in him.

He ascended Stemster Hill and wandered about the summit where some of Graysteel's retainers at the castle would be sure to see him and go and inform their master. When he saw some activity around the castle walls, he began to walk down the hill towards the castle. He was about two or three hundred yards away when Graysteel came forth in warlike array, complete with drawn sword and shield.

Graysteel bellowed: "You have dared to trespass on my land. Draw your sword so that you may make an attempt to defend yourself before I kill you. You know that no person leaves this land alive."

"Villain!" cried Dunn, unsheathing the sword, which flashed in the sun. "You wantonly slew my friend and this day you shall pay for it with your heart's blood." Graysteel laughed at what he thought was empty bravado.

"Your body will join that of your friend in the loch," he shouted.

He made a thrust at Dunn with his sword, which was expertly parried. A bitter struggle ensued and Graysteel used all his speed and skill, but Dunn defended himself with amazing precision. The clang of steel echoed the hills as Dunn blocked every move made by his opponent's sword. Graysteel circled his opponent like an enraged lion and then struck savagely only to find that Dunn's defences could not be penetrated. Here was the king of all the swordsmen fighting a losing battle against a mere youth! He grew more and more bewildered and enraged.

Suddenly, he let out a roar and grasped his shoulder, trying to feign a serious injury; but Dunn stood and smiled, waiting to strike again. Even more infuriated, Graysteel struck a vicious blow with his sword. It was parried with such force that it was almost wrenched from his hand. Before Graysteel could regain his balance, Dunn had thrust his sword through the black heart of his opponent. With a great roar that echoed through the hills, Graysteel threw his hands in the air and fell dead in the heather.

Graysteel's retainers were so bewildered by the death of their leader that they never thought to pursue Dunn, who escaped over the hills back to his own castle.

He gathered all his retainers and returned with them to Loch Rangag where, after a brief struggle, he took the castle. Dunn dealt mercifully with Graysteel's retainers, but after they were all out of the castle he ordered his followers to tear down the walls. The ruin of the castle today is said to be much as when Dunn left it.

Dunn went back to the cottage in Halsary and returned the widow's sword. She was overjoyed when she heard that Graysteel was dead. He offered her a house at Dunn and promised that he would provide for her for the rest of her days. She gladly accepted this offer and, before he took her to Dunn, he drove her in a carriage to Loch Rangag where she saw the ruins of Graysteel's castle. Looking across the quiet waters of the loch, she said, "Loch Rangag has been known throughout the world as a place of violence through the wicked deeds of Graysteel. Now that he is dead, may peace forever prevail on this beautiful loch."

Today, visitors to Loch Rangag, regarded as one of the beauty spots of Caithness, may feel that the wish of the widow has been fulfilled.

Dunn gave the widow a cottage near his castle, where he cared for her for the rest of her life. A few months later he was united in marriage with the beautiful Miss Sinclair of Rattar. The ceremony was attended by people from all over Caithness, who regarded Dunn as their deliverer from the fear of Graysteel, and among the special guests was the widow from Halsary.

The ruins of Graysteel's Castle at Loch Rangag

The Dairymaid and the Hunter

FROM THE BEGINNING OF TIME, tales of romance and the supernatural have enhanced our lives. Our forefathers wrapped a golden thread of romance around their lives and we can only learn of it by singing their songs and telling their stories. The shielings in the olden days were the places where these songs and stories survived. When finished with the milking at the end of the day, one of the youthful maidens would sing one of the songs and then one of the men would tell the story or legend behind the song. In this way the nights were spent in the bothies in a pleasant manner, which in some ways seems to be superior to life today. One of the most popular songs sung in the shielings in the Highlands of Caithness was a Gaelic lament, the English translation of which was *Miss Calder's Lament.* This song was said to bring tears to the listeners' eyes as it resounded through the shielings at the end of the day.

The legend of the song is as follows: late in the sixteenth or early in the seventeenth century, Donald MacKay, the Strathnaver Chief of the Clan MacKay, had a son named Ian Ban Mar. Ian had a dispute with some of his clan in Strathnaver, and was forced to leave with his wife and children and come to Caithness. He moved around Caithness for some time, but eventually settled at Dalnawillan, which is situated among the hills in the parish of Halkirk.

Ian was a powerful man of great ability and, like most men of his time, was a great hunter. In those days, out in the lonely moorland, people had a difficult task to tell the different days of the week, and were always afraid of incurring the wrath of the ministers and the kirk session, if they should encroach on the Sabbath day. Ian soon became a great favourite with all his neighbours, and as he was a deeply religious man, he devised a plan which would put his neighbours' minds at ease, so they could not be confused with the Sabbath day. On Sundays, Ian dressed himself in his scarlet hunting cloak, climbed to the top of Ben Alisky, and stood on the summit so that all his neighbours would know the day of the week. In this way Ian and his neighbours were on good terms with the ministers.

One day while Ian was out hunting in the hills around Dalnawillan, he found a baby boy sound asleep in a neuk in the heather. Ian immediately believed that the child had been left there by the fairies, and as the child was, like him, a stranger in a strange land, he thought that it was put there to test his reaction. He gazed upon the sleeping form of the child and thought of the words of the Bible: "Unless you become as a little child, you shall not enter into the Kingdom of Heaven." Ian carefully lifted the child in his arms and carried him to his home, where his wife and family looked after him. Ian already had a family of two daughters and three sons, but he immediately decided that he should bring this baby up as his foster-son.

The child grew up to be very strong, and Ian believed that he must have been descended from some race of giants. He had a natural aptitude for hunting and, when still a boy, became an excellent archer. Wrestling was part of every young boy's training at that time, and Ian gave instruction in this art to his foster-son, but it was not long before he could out-wrestle his foster-father. Ian was so delighted with the boy's performance that he called a great gathering of people, and had the boy baptised Na Gille Garbh, or the brave lad.

Gille Garbh loved to hunt on the hills and became so successful a hunter that he was able to provide for his family when he was still a boy, and while he was doing this Ian Ban Mor was able to take life easy. He believed that this was a reward for the compassion he had shown to the baby whom he had found on the hills.

At that time a large family of Calders owned the farm of Achnacly in Dunbeath Strath. The family consisted of twelve sons and several daughters. One of the daughters was gifted with exceptional beauty, and was known as the Flower of Achnacly. This daughter and several other young maidens were sent out with cattle to a shieling near Ben Alisky. When the Gille Garbh was out hunting he often called in at this shieling and spent a pleasant time in the company of the maidens. On his first visit to the shieling he was greatly struck by the beauty of Miss Calder. She had long dark hair and her skin was whiter than driven snow. He was so attracted by her beauty that he made every excuse that he could think of to visit the shieling. She, in turn, was drawn towards the Gille Garbh, and it was not long before they fell in love. Some of the people at the shieling mentioned to her father that she was keeping company with the Gille Garbh, and he immediately forbade her to be seen in his company. She tried to argue with her father that the Gille Garbh was a nice young man, but he immediately ordered her to have no association with him as long as she was a daughter of his. Miss Calder and the Gille Garbh continued to see each other by arranging secret meetings in the hills.

Her father employed a herd by the name of Magnus Gunn, who was small in stature, and rather strange looking, with a desperate desire for money and riches. The lovers made an agreement with Magnus that they would elope into the hills under the cover of darkness and take the pick of the herd of cattle with them. On a beautiful autumn night when the hills were illuminated by the moon, Magnus collected a number of cattle, and he and the lovers began their journey. They drove the cattle into the hills, keeping west of the district of Braemore, and continued on until they came to Kildonan in Sutherland. Here they chose a secluded dell beside a burn where they built a bothy. They enjoyed life in their new surroundings, where their love blossomed like a rose. Magnus tended their cattle on the hills, and life for them was pleasant and sweet.

Magnus had a wife who lived in Dunbeath Strath, and he used to make secret visits to her during the night, so that he would not be seen by any of the Calders who were vowing vengeance on the Gille Garbh for the loss of their cattle. The Calder brothers made vile threats towards the Gille Garbh, but at heart they were afraid to come face to face with him because of his renown as an archer and a swordsman.

One moonlit night while Magnus was journeying through the hills to Dunbeath Strath to visit his wife, he was suddenly confronted by one of the Calder brothers who had seen Magnus approach, and hidden in the heather. Magnus was filled with horror when he saw that he was trapped, but Calder soon allayed his fears by being very friendly towards him. Magnus always believed that he was as good as dead if he met any of his employer's sons in the hills, but this young man bade him sit down on the heather and have a chat.

"How would you like to be rich?" asked young Calder. "I will never be rich," replied Magnus.

"If you will assist me and my brothers, you can easily be one of the richest men in Dunbeath Strath. You know that the Gille Garbh and my sister stole the best of our cattle and has left our family poor. If you will betray the Gille Garbh, you can have two thirds of the cattle stolen by him."

Magnus was a man of low character and the thought of money and riches immediately made his face flush, as he would creep to any depth for the love of money. "I will do my best to help you," stammered Magnus. The thought of riches had put his mind in a complete whirl, and all that he could think of was some ploy to destroy his master, the Gille Garbh, so that he could become rich. The words of the Bible which said, what would it profit a man if he should gain the whole world, and lose his own soul, meant nothing to Magnus. Magnus was going to be rich and self-respect or love meant nothing to him as long as he achieved his aim.

Calder told Magnus that after he returned to the Gille Garbh's bothy in Kildonan on an appointed night, when his master was asleep, he was to cut his master's bowstring, and also all the spare bowstrings. This would leave the Gille Garbh without his most devastating weapon, and he would then be easy prey to Calder and his eleven brothers. Magnus readily agreed to do this, as all he could think about was riches.

On the appointed night, when the Gille Garbh was asleep, Magnus rose and cut the string in his master's bow with a corkag, a small knife. He also cut all the spare strings for the bow.

The Gille Garbh woke early that morning as he was having troubled dreams and a short time later heard noises outside the bothy. He immediately went to the window and saw the twelve Calder brothers approach. He went for his bow, but alas! it was useless. He then went for the spare strings and found that they had also been cut, so he knew that he had been betrayed by his herd. The Gille Garbh then went to where Magnus was lying sound asleep and said: "Ill it was for me that you had a corkag." He then struck Magnus a severe blow which laid him prostrate for ever. Without a weapon to defend himself, he knew there was nothing left for him but death at the hands of his assailants. He went to his loved one, and kissed her good-bye for ever. She asked him to try and make his escape by crossing the burn and then try to disappear among the heather in the hills. In a final effort to make good his escape, he made a dash across the burn, but was cut down by a hail of arrows from the Calders' bows. When his loved one looked out, she saw him lying dead in a pool of blood, with her cruel brothers standing over him.

Miss Calder would have nothing to do with her cruel brothers and remained in the bothy where she and the Gille Garbh had been so happy. Before the brothers drove off her cattle, they buried the body of the Gille Garbh near the spot where he had been killed. The treacherous Magnus Gunn received no burial, and this was said to be one of the greatest insults that could be conferred on the remains of any person. By treachery he had tried to secure riches, but he only lost his low life. Miss Calder was so overcome with grief that she never recovered, but before she died she wrote this beautiful lament for her loved one:

On our herd may a thousand vile curses descend,
In his last winding shroud where they've laid him;
Who came to our home, and my lover, alas!
To my bloodthirsty brothers betrayed him.

If only but two of my brothers had come
You might only take time to awaken;
Yes, even to four, you were equal to them,
But twelve had thy strength overtaken.

My eyes never looked on a figure so grand,
Thy features they shone with a light eye,
Thou always stood forth 'mong the brave of the land,
And a hero thou went 'mong the mighty!

When Ian with his bow in his strong and sure hand,
Went a-hunting o'er mountains so wild,
He found thee cradled away in the moorland,
A brave and beautiful child.

Like two lovely flowerlets we were to the view
In a cliff of a mountain alone,
And there from one root our tender lives grew,
Can I live when that root is gone?

Why should I love you so dearly my dear one?
Because there was one soul within us,
Then how can I live without you
And dark death forever between us?

With thy corkag, oh Magnus! you did it,
With a vile and treacherous move,
Why did not kind fate forbid it?
The act that brought death to my love.

How blithe would I live with my dearie,
Far away in lone Bothan Airaidh,
With none to disturb or to steer thee,
Save the birds in the groves and the corrie.

Thy life's sun shone bright in the morning,
No sorrow beclouded its light;
Now the clouds of death hang heavily mourning
The sun which on Morven is set!

A short time after this some of the Calder's horses went missing in the hills around Ben Alisky. Four of the sons who were armed with crossbows went out to look for them. When they were passing Ian Ban Mor's house at Dalnawillan in the early morning, one of them fired an arrow through the window of the house, hoping that Ian would be seated in his chair just inside the window. However, luck was with Ian, as he was away with his sons. When he returned to his home, and was told of the desperate attempt which had been made on his life by the Calders, he immediately armed himself, and accompanied by his three sons, set off in pursuit.

After travelling a short distance, Ian was told that the Calders had broken up; two of them had gone towards Altnabreac, while the other two had gone up the Thurso River. Ian and one of his sons followed the two Calders towards Altnabreac, while the other two sons followed the Calders up the Thurso River.

Ian and his son overtook the Calders at a loch a short distance west of Altnabreac. A fierce battle ensued, but the Calders were not able to stand up for long against the onslaught of Ian and his son, and it was not long before they fell mortally wounded. Ian carried the bodies of his enemies home to Dalnawillan and had them buried on the hill above the house where the present cemetery stands.

The other two Calder brothers were overtaken by Ian's two sons at a place called Lenn-Na-Cat, which is a waterfall on the Thurso River, about two miles west of Glutt. The Calders put up a desperate fight, but in the end they were slain by Ian's sons. They are said to have been buried in a nearby chapel.

Ian Ban Mor got his revenge on four of the twelve brothers who had treacherously slain his foster-son, the Gille Garbh, but it is through the beautiful medium of music that Miss Calder really perpetuated his memory.

The Writing on the Wall
A Legend of Girnigoe Castle

VISITORS TO GIRNIGOE CASTLE WILL notice the words 'Nae Hope' and the date 1635 are carved on a stone in the wall of the dungeon. The number 5 is partly obliterated, but it is believed that the date is 1635. The general belief that these words were carved by the Master of Caithness before he was starved to death by his father in the dungeon in 1576 is not the case.

About 1629 a south country gentleman by the name of Sir Dudley Merton was shipwrecked near Oldwick Castle, Caithness. He was given help and shelter by Sir Hugh Oliphant who resided in the castle. Sir Dudley was just over twenty years of age at the time, and was greatly attracted by the beauty and charm of Sir Hugh's daughter, Norma, who was then 18 years of age. Sir Hugh did not encourage their courtship, and when he found that they were on intimate terms, he dispatched Sir Dudley to his home. He had plans for Norma marrying the Earl of Caithness, who was about 60 years of age.

The marriage was duly arranged, and although Norma protested, she was forced to go through with it, as it would improve her father's position in Caithness to have the Earl as his son-in-law. Norma was never happy as the Countess of Caithness with the old Earl as her husband, and yearned for her true love, Sir Dudley. An only son was born about a year after the marriage.

Six years later, Sir Dudley Merton returned to Caithness, and paid a secret visit to the Countess at Girnigoe Castle, when the Earl and his

Sinclair and Girnigoe Castles. Girnigoe Castle is on the right of the photograph

young son were out sailing in a war galley. The Countess pleaded with Sir Dudley not to renew their old affair because of the danger of them being found out by the Earl, but at the same time she let him know that she was very much in love with him.

The Earl and his party returned unexpectedly to the castle, and found Sir Dudley with the Countess. Sir Dudley put up a desperate fight for his life, in which he wounded two of the retainers, but in the end he was overpowered. Sir Dudley was locked in the dungeon, and the Countess was locked in her room. The Earl kept the key attached to his belt, as he was afraid that some of the staff might set her free.

One of the staff, Rory Gunn, who had previously been employed by Sir Hugh Oliphant at Oldwick Castle, had great respect for the Countess, so he devised a plan to set her free. One day, as the Earl was preparing to leave on one of his cruises, he accidentally bumped into him and was able to unhook the key. After the Earl and his party left, he released the Countess from her room and then endeavoured to escape from the castle without alerting the guards, or using the drawbridge.

Rory noticed that there was a small rowing boat moored at the water's edge, near the end of the secret passage through the rock from the castle.

This boat was always left as a means of escape for the Earl in the event of the castle being attacked from the landward side. Rory and the Countess slipped unnoticed from the castle and boarded the boat. They intended to row to Oldwick Castle where she would get help and protection from her father. Rory and the Countess had only rowed a short distance around the bay, when they were spotted by the Earl and his party on board his war galley. The Earl was so infuriated that the Countess should attempt to escape, he immediately ordered the captain in charge of the war galley to run down the rowing boat. Norma and Rory were both thrown into the sea when their boat was smashed by the galley. The Earl ordered that no person should go to their aid, and they were both left in the sea until they were drowned.

The Earl, who was very cruel, was pleased that he had disposed of his Countess. He returned to the castle to have vengeance on her lover. He ordered that neither food nor water should be given to Sir Dudley Merton, so that he would die a slow and painful death for having dared to try and steal the Countess of Caithness. Sir Dudley was confined to the dungeon, and as his hopes and strength began to fade, he carved the words 'Nae Hope, 1635' on a stone in the wall. The inscription remains as a memorial to the wickedness of the Earl of Caithness. Sir Dudley died a few days after he had completed the inscription from raging hunger and thirst.

The Battle of Altimarlach

GEORGE SINCLAIR, THE SIXTH EARL of Caithness, died in 1676, and had no male heir to succeed him. Before his death he was in grave financial difficulties, so he sold his estates, title and all, to Lord Glenorchy, who was one of his principal creditors. There were two dispositions in favour of Glenorchy, the first dated June 10 1661, and the second dated October 8 1672, conveying all the lands and property. The second disposition stated that in the event of non-redemption, Glenorchy and his heirs would be able to assume the surname Sinclair, and wear the arms of Caithness.

Glenorchy was known as The Grey Fox, and there can be no doubt that he tricked the Earl of Caithness to put his name in this disposition. For the remainder of his life George Sinclair received an annuity of two thousand merks from Glenorchy.

Sinclair's wife was a daughter of the Earl of Argyle, and a relation of Glenorchy, and after Sinclair died in 1676, Glenorchy married his widow, the then Dowager Countess. He assumed the title Earl of Caithness. By this time the deed under which he acquired the estates had been confirmed by Royal Charter under the Great Seal.

The method by which Glenorchy had acquired the Earldom did not help his popularity in Caithness, and many of the landlords despised him. In order to have at least one influential friend in the county, he appointed Sir John Sinclair of Murkle, Sherriff and Justiciary Depute of Caithness, and also made him Baillie of the Baronies on the Caithness estate.

George Sinclair of Keiss, son of Francis Sinclair of Northfield, disputed Glenorchy's right to the title. He also disputed his right to the lands of Northfield and Tister which he had inherited from his father. The dispute was eventually submitted to four of the most distinguished lawyers in Scotland at that time, namely: Sir George Sinclair, Sir Robert Sinclair of Longformacus, Sir George Lochart, and Sir John Cunningham. Their decision was in favour of Glenorchy, and it was sent to the King.

There can be no doubt that the Grey Fox's money had influenced the lawyers in their decision. The King sent a letter to the Privy Council, ordering them to issue a proclamation prohibiting George Sinclair of Keiss from assuming the title Earl of Caithness.

Sinclair paid no attention to this interdict, and retained possession of his lands. He also took every opportunity to enrage Glenorchy's chamberlains, making it difficult for them to collect their rents. Most of the gentlemen in the county did not actively support Sinclair's cause, although in general they were sympathetic towards him, and looked upon Glenorchy as a person who had cheated the late Earl out of his possessions.

Two of Sinclair's friends, David Sinclair of Broynach and William Sinclair of Thura, gave him all the assistance he required. Glenorchy had taken possession of Thurso Castle, so George Sinclair and a party attacked it and succeeded in nearly demolishing it. Glenorchy appealed to the Privy Council that George Sinclair had failed to obey the interdict. On November 11, 1679, the Privy Council passed an Act charging the hail kin, friends and followers of John, Earl of Caithness, to concur and assist in recovering the disputed lands.

In order to put this Act into effect in the summer of 1680, Glenorchy invaded Caithness with one thousand one hundred men. The force was made up of the different branches of the Clan Campbell, including Glenlyon, Glenfalloch, Glendochart and Achallander, together with men from the estates of his brother-in-law, the Laird of Macnab.

Glenorchy's men were passing through Braemore on the confines of the county, when George Sinclair was informed of their presence. He immediately made plans to meet Glenorchy in the open field and collected all his followers. Some accounts say that he had 500 men, while others say that he had 800. His force consisted of a number of old men, and they were all totally untrained for the proposed encounter. The only person with military training was William Sinclair of Thura, who had served as a major in the German wars.

The two armies met near Stirkoke, but as it was near night, and as the Grey Fox Glenorchy had other plans afoot, he declined battle and retired to the hills of Yarrows. The place where the Campbells spent the night was known as Torran na Gael, or the Highlander's Hill. Glenorchy's main reason for declining battle with the Sinclairs was that he did not intend to have a fair fight, but was planning some sort of ambush, or element of surprise. He or some of his officers would be surveying the land around Stirkoke for a spot that would serve their purpose.

The Burn of Altimarlach joins the north side of the Wick River about two and a half miles west of the town, below Stirkoke. This is a rather strange watercourse, as it runs for only a distance of two to three hundred yards, when it dries up almost completely. Near where it joins the Wick River it has steep banks which form a deep gulley. The land beside the burn is high and then slopes away towards the river, forming a peninsula. The Grey Fox, or some of his officers, must have thought the burn of Altimarlach an ideal site for the forthcoming battle.

The Sinclairs retired to Wick where Glenorchy had an unusual party awaiting them. He had arranged that one of his ships laden with whisky should go aground near the mouth of the Wick River. A secret agent of the Campbells gave some of the whisky to the Sinclairs. They then took possession of the ship and spent the night in riotous drinking. The Campbells, however, acted more prudently and Glenorchy appointed strict guards around the hills in case of a surprise attack. The rest of his men wrapped themselves in their plaids and slept soundly in the heather.

Early next morning, July 13, Glenorchy left the hills of Yarrows with his army and marched to Stirkoke where he crossed the Wick River below Stirkoke Mains about eight o'clock in the morning. His men are said to have leaped across, and from the narrowness of the stream at some points it does not seem impossible. The news that Glenorchy's army was on the move soon reached Wick, where George Sinclair had great difficulty mustering his men from their drunken stupors. Then, in great disarray he led them up the river to meet the enemy.

Glenorchy had prepared for battle some time earlier. He drew up five hundred of his men on the flat ground beside the river, about two hundred yards up from where it is joined by the Burn of Altimarlach. He ordered the rest of his men to conceal themselves in the gulley of the burn, and not to move until their officers ordered them to do so. While awaiting the arrival of the Sinclairs, he delivered this address in Gaelic: "We are this day in enemy's country. He that stands by me, I'll stand by him, my son by his son, and my grandson by his grandson; but if this day goes against us, he will be a lucky man that ever gets home, for far is the cry to Lochawe, and far is the help from Cruachan."

When the Sinclairs arrived, they made a detour to the right at some distance at the head of the gulley and did not see the ambush that was laid for them. The detour was made in order to get the advantage of higher ground and to keep the enemy between them and the river.

Once the armies were a short distance apart, Glenorchy gave the signal for the attack, and the battle commenced. The Campbells charged furiously against the Sinclairs, and, weak as they were after their night of pleasure, their lines gave way and they were driven before the broadswords of the Campbells up the brae towards the Burn of Altimarlach. The reserves of the Campbells rose up from their ambush in the gorge, and met the Sinclairs in the face.

The Sinclairs were now pressed from the front and the rear, so, in a last desperate bid to escape, they rushed downhill towards the river. The Campbells chased them into the water and cut them down with their broadswords. So many were slain that the Campbells were able to walk over the river dry-shod on the bodies of the Sinclairs. A number of the Sinclairs who endeavoured to escape by making a rush for the open plain were cut down by the battle axes and broadswords of the Campbells. Sinclair of Feiss, Sinclair of Thura, and other leaders of the party who were on horseback, were able to escape, owing to the fleetness of their horses. The battle did not last more than a few minutes, but in this short time more than two hundred of the Caithness men died.

The battle of Altimarlach ended in disaster for the county of Caithness, and was a humiliating blow to the pride of the Sinclairs. During the heat of the battle, when the Caithness men were beginning to give way, Finlay

McIver, Glenorchy's piper, struck up a tune which seemed to express the Gaelic words, *Bodach na briogais*. This may be translated as *The Bodies with the Breeks*, and was a sarcastic way of referring to the trousers worn by the Sinclairs. The tune has been handed down to modern times, and is now known as *The Caries with the Breeks*. McIver is also said to have composed the tunes, *The Campbells are Coming* and *The Hills of Glenorchy*, on the way to Altimarlach.

After the battle, Glenorchy quartered some of his troops in Caithness. They levied rents and taxes on the inhabitants, and in general treated them very harshly and oppressively, as if in a conquered country. The remainder of his men were sent home in detached companies. With the last company went the chief bard and piper, Finlay McIver. The weather was very warm, and in order to quench their thirst before crossing the Ord of Caithness, the party called at the public house at Milton, Dunbeath, then famed for its superior quality of ale. The Highlanders were so delighted with the drink that they stayed there celebrating for two days. They then left for home, leaving Finlay McIver behind.

He had spent all his money, and in order to settle his debt, the landlady had taken possession of his bagpipes. He pleaded with her to have his pipes returned, but out of sympathy for the defeated Sinclairs, she turned a deaf ear to all his pleas. Finlay was in a sore plight and felt much worse than if Glenorchy had been defeated by the Bodies with the Breeks; and the disgrace would have been nothing compared to the loss of his pipes in such circumstances.

However, William Roy McIver, one of Glenorchy's factors who lived near Dunbeath, heard of Finlay's predicament. He came to the inn, paid all Finlay's debt, and asked that the pipes should be restored to their rightful owner. "Now my good fellow," said the factor, clapping Finlay on the shoulder and handing him enough money to pay for his expenses on the way home, "I hope that you will be a little more moderate in your drinking in future and not get in such a fix again, at least before you reach the braes of Glenorchy, for, mind you, I will not always be at hand to redeem the pipes."

Finlay was too overjoyed to express his gratitude in words to the factor, so he composed a beautiful Gaelic song in his honour and named it *Failt*

The Old Inn at Milton, Dunbeath Strath. It was here that some of Glenorchy's men celebrated for two days after the battle.

Clan Ibhair. The factor was very pleased with the song, which recorded his good qualities and it is said it was never sung in his company without him treating the company to half an anker of brandy. The song survived as long as Gaelic was spoken in the Highlands of Caithness.

Undaunted by his reverse at Altimarlach, George Sinclair of Keiss continued his opposition to Glenorchy. He laid siege to Castle Sinclair and took it after feeble resistance was put up by the defenders. For this he and his three friends, Sinclair of Broynach, Sinclair of Thura and MacKay of Strathnaver fell under the ban of the Government and were declared rebels. Afterwards, through the influence of the Duke of York, later James II, George Sinclair finally secured his claim to the Earldom of Caithness and obtained possession of his patrimonial property.

The sale of the Earldom was classed as an illegal transaction, and the decision of the Scottish lawyers in favour of Glenorchy seems very strange. The Earldom of Caithness was a male fee by its original grant, which would seem to be a bar in any way for it being gifted or disposed of to a stranger, and even of the King altering its tenure, where there was no previous forfeiture.

Glenorchy was Earl of Caithness for about six years, and as compensation for his loss of title was created Earl of Breadalbane and Baron of Wick. He was detested by the natives of Caithness, who regarded him as a military butcher, and never forgave him for the slaughter of their friends at Altimarlach. They took every opportunity of annoying him and his successor. In 1719 he sold the estates in Caithness to Sinclair of Ulbster.

Glenorchy was described as being grave as a Spaniard, wise as a serpent, cunning as a fox and slippery as an eel. By his dealings in Caithness, he seems to have well earned these descriptions. In 1692 he became implicated in organising the Massacre of Glencoe, and for this treacherous deed an action of High Treason was raised against him. He was committed to prison in Edinburgh, where he remained for some time, but was eventually released without being brought to trial

The site of the battle of Altimarlach is marked by a Celtic cross which bears the following inscription: 'The Battle of Altimarlach was fought around this spot, 13th July 1680. The last feudal battle in Scotland. Erected 1901'.

The inscription on the cross is not correct as it was not the last feudal battle in Scotland. The last recorded clan battle in Scotland was the battle of Mulroy in Inverness-shire, which was fought between the clans Macintosh and the MacDonalds of Keppoch on 4th August, 1688. It ended in victory for the Macintoshes. Altimarlach can be termed as one of the last clan battles in Scotland.

The Celtic cross on the site of the Battle of Altimarlach, with a view towards the town of Wick.

John Finlaison
Actuary of the National Debt
Court and Government Calculator

STATISTICS ARE NOW OBTAINED FROM information fed into a computer, but if we look back through the dim mists of time it will be interesting to learn something of a Scotsman who was the first computator employed by the British Government. John Finlayson, or Finlaison as he later spelt his name, who was the first Government Calculator, was born in a humble fisherman's cottage in the north of Scotland, but by his own skill and determination rose to one of the top jobs in London.

John Finlayson was the eldest son of Donald Finlayson and his wife Isabella Sutherland. He was born in Thurso, Caithness on 27th August, 1783. Donald Finlayson in his early life was employed as a sailor in the coasting trade, but after his marriage he returned to Thurso where he settled down as a fisherman. He had three of a family: John was the oldest, a daughter named Christian was second, and William was the youngest.

When John was seven years of age, his father contracted brain fever and died on 28th November, 1790, aged 29 years, leaving his wife and family unprovided for, Christian was three years of age at the time and William was only four months. Mrs Finlayson faced the bereavement with Christian fortitude, and worked hard to bring up her family. There were no funds available at that time to help widows, other than a small payment from the poor funds of the parish church, but the neighbours rallied round to help families who had bereavements, such was the community spirit in the north of Scotland at that time. She was a woman of careful and industrious habits, and although she often had to go with very little food for herself, she always tried to get the best for her family. She also made it clear that she did not wish her sons to follow the dangerous calling of fishermen, and made them take every opportunity that was available for education.

John attended the parish school where he was taught by William Munro. Munro, who later became the Rev. William Munro, was an accomplished scholar, and instilled in his pupils a love of the classics. John Finlayson showed a great aptitude for learning and soon became a favourite with his teacher. He was good at English, geography and history, but in the field of mathematics he was something of a genius. Books and study were more attractive to him than the boyish games of his companions. At night he was content to stay in the house studying while his companions played games. His mother was delighted that he was doing so well at school, and encouraged him in every way.

When John was 15 years of age he left school and started an apprenticeship with Mr Robeson, a solicitor in Thurso. Shortly after he started his apprenticeship, he took an interest in music and began studying the theory and practice of it. The flute was his favourite instrument, and he often spent his leisure hours playing it.

Finlayson served an apprenticeship of four years with Mr Robeson, after which he was appointed factor on Sir Benjamin Dunbar's estate at Ackergill, near Wick. He spent about two years as factor there. In August 1804 he relinquished his appointment and went to Edinburgh. The big cities had always held an attraction for Finlayson, and he knew he would not spend the rest of his life in Caithness without sampling life in the big cities.

In Edinburgh he secured a situation as a clerk with Mr Glen, Writer to the Signet. His stay in Edinburgh lasted for only a few weeks, but it so happened that he met his wife in the most unusual circumstances. Finlayson was invited to dinner at his employer's house, and it so happened that Mr Glen's sister's seat at the table was near the fire and during the dinner party her dress accidentally caught fire. Most of the people at the dinner panicked and did not know what to do so the young lady was in danger of being consumed by the flames. Finlayson showed his initiative in this desperate situation, and immediately pulled the table cover off the table, wrapped it round the young lady and extinguished the fire. The lady did not know how to thank her youthful rescuer and shortly afterwards another fire was kindled between them, the everlasting fire of love. When Mr Glen found that his young sister was associating with his young clerk, he immediately forbade them to see each other again. The tender pang of love had already grown too strong for Miss Glen or Mr Finlayson to be persuaded by the angry words of Mr Glen, so they eloped to London in September 1804, and were married there.

In 1805 Finlayson obtained employment as a clerk in the Admiralty. He soon distinguished himself in his new employment by putting forward a plan for the reorganisation of the system under which the entire correspondence of the department was carried on. Finlayson's plan was adopted, and was found to be a vast improvement on the old system. The navy list was also compiled by him.

After Finlayson obtained employment in London he changed the spelling of his name to Finlaison. He also arranged for an annuity to be paid to his mother so that the closing years of her life were spent in comfort. About the same time he procured a Midshipman's Commission for his brother William who had joined the Navy at the age of fifteen years, and was serving on H.M.S. *Beagle* under Captain Fitzroy. William had accompanied Captain Fitzroy round the world on a voyage of scientific discovery. This voyage took almost four years to complete.

In 1817, while working on the establishment of a widows' fund for the civil service and widows of Navy Medical Officers, Finlaison's attention was drawn to the study of vital statistics. The information then available was very meagre and unsatisfactory. He examined the records of the Chancellor of the Exchequer on certain classes of annuities which had been paid out. He then made certain new deductions from authentic information which enabled him to successfully point out that the tables used by the government for the distribution of annuities were inadequate. Finlaison's representations were favourably received by Mr Vansittart, Chancellor of the Exchequer, who adopted the new system which made a huge saving to the country.

The new system introduced by Finlaison was a tremendous success, and as a result of this he was appointed the first Government Actuary in 1821. From this time on his counsel and calculating powers were put to use when any of the public measures introduced by the Government required mathematics. He was involved with the Bank of England in the negotiations for the Bank accepting the charge of the public pensions.

In 1825 and 1827 he advised select committees of the House of Commons into the general condition of friendly societies. In 1829 he prepared a report on the evidence and elementary facts on which his new tables for friendly societies were founded. This was an important Parliamentary document which contained twenty-one new views on the law of mortality, one on the law of sickness prevailing among the labouring classes in London, vast tables of the duration of slave and creole life, it also referred to the possible emancipation of slaves in 1834, and the West Indian loan to be raised for that purpose. Finlaison's report on Mr Hume's resolutions on that loan is a paper well worth reading. In 1835 he was adviser to the Ecclesiastical Commission which was set up and was responsible for a number of reforms in the English Church.

During the negotiations for the setting up of the compulsory registration of births, deaths, and marriages in 1837, Finlaison's dexterity as a calculator really came out. He made an estimate of the number of deaths which would be registered in the first year, and it was proven to be correct to within fourteen in a total of almost 330,000. This caused a great sensation when the Registrar General's first annual report was published, and it clearly shows that Finlaison was no ordinary calculator.

Finlaison's first wife died during the 1830s and he later married a second time to a Miss Davies who was a native of Buckinghamshire. He had a family by his first wife but the number is not known.

In 1842, while Finlaison was visiting an exhibition of electrical instruments at the Polytechnic Institution, London, he was greatly impressed by an electrical printing telegraph which was on exhibition. On making further enquiries about it, he was informed that it had been invented by a young man named Alexander Bain, who was a native of Watten, Caithness. Finlaison immediately went and spoke to him and, shortly afterwards, a great friendship developed between them. Bain had at that time invented an electric clock, as well as the printing telegraph, but was being greatly harassed by Professor Charles Wheatstone, who had disputed his rights to claim patents for his inventions. Wheatstone had tried to claim that the electric clock and the printing telegraph were his inventions, and not Bain's. Finlaison being an honest and trustworthy person, immediately took up Bain's cause, and helped and advised him in his claim for his later patents. Bain, assisted by Finlaison, proved to be more than a match for Wheatstone in the years that followed. In 1843 Finlaison wrote a book entitled *An Account of Some of the Memorable Applications of the Electric Fluid by A. Bain*. Bain was a regular visitor to Finlaison's house in Epping Forest, where he carried out some of his important experiments, and it was there that he discovered that the earth could be used as a return path for electricity. He became friendly with Finlaison's wife's sister, Matilda Davies, or Bowie, a young widow, and they later married. Bain is recognised as the inventor of the electric clock, the electric printing telegraph, and also has many more lesser-known patents in the fields of electrical horology and telegraphy.

Bain was one of the electrical geniuses of the world, but if it was not for the intervention of John Finlaison on his behalf, he could well have been crushed by Wheatstone at the beginning of his career.

Finlaison was frequently called upon to give evidence before Royal Commissioners and Select Committees of both Houses of Parliament. The strenuous demands made upon his mental powers finally affected his health, and his doctor advised him to cut down on his work. He continued to work in a limited scope as Actuary to the National Debt Court and Government Calculator until he finally retired in August, 1851, aged 68 years. The last years of his work as Government Calculator were taken up with scripture chronology and the relationship of ancient and modern weights and measures. His researches into weights and measures were very deep, and this led him to oppose the introduction of decimal coinage and metrology into this country at that time. Finlaison possessed extraordinary abilities as an accountant and, before his retirement, was recognised as the most expert calculator in the world.

The last years of Finlaison's life were spent in some ease and tranquillity at his home in Notting Hill, London. He eventually contracted congestion of the lungs and died at his house on 13th August, 1860, aged 76 years.

His brother William Finlayson rose to the rank of Commander in the Royal Navy. After he retired, he was appointed Governor of the island of Ascension. The climate affected his health and he was forced to relinquish this post. He died in 1851, aged 61 years.

The Strong Man of Dalnaglaton

IN 1758, THE WIFE OF George Gunn, Dalnaglaton, Caithness, gave birth to a son. The child was so small and weak that he had to be rolled in sheep's wool and a basket was used as a cradle. Nobody believed that this weakling would survive, but his mother was very religious and prayed to God to give her poor child strength, and tended the child with extra loving care.

After a few days the baby began to put on weight and grow stronger. His mother fully believed that his recovery was not an earthly act, but was guided from above. Every morning and night she gave thanks to God in her prayers.

The child was baptised Alexander, and soon became a strong, healthy baby, much admired by everyone. When he grew to boyhood, he was bigger and stronger than all the others of his age in the district. He showed great promise as an athlete, and could out-run and out-jump lads much older than himself.

One day, his mother sent him and his younger brother to cut firewood. While they were away, a bull, which was grazing near the house, went mad and tried to attack her. She escaped only by climbing on to the roof of the house, but she was in terror for the lives of her two young boys as they would soon be returning. Presently, she saw the boys walking towards the house. She shouted a warning to them, but at that very moment the bull saw them and charged. Alexander told his brother to run, and lifting a branch he was carrying, struck the bull a heavy blow on the back, paralysing the animal. The bull died a short time later and when its carcase was examined, every rib was found to be broken.

When Alexander grew up he was noted for his quiet good nature and phenomenal strength. He possessed the strength of a lion, but was said to be as gentle as a Iamb. He was the friend of the weak and oppressed, and protected them from the bullies who were prevalent at that time. Alexander was just and upright in all his dealings, thanks to his religious upbringing.

One day, while out hunting with some friends near the Thurso River above The Glutt, Alexander decided to cross to the other bank. One of his friends dared him to jump across a gulley, above the waterfall called *Essabadienabeig*. The precipitous rocks on the south side of the gulley are called *Creighe a' Chait*, the Jump of the Cat. The rocks on the south side are about twenty-five feet high, while those on the other side are only five. Alexander immediately accepted the challenge, and after taking a short, quick run towards the south side of the gulley, cleared it with a flying leap.

One day, Alexander and his servant went to a market in Thurso. Alexander entered one of the refreshment tents, leaving his servant outside holding his silver cane. A well-known bully, Thomas Munro from the Western Isles, who was known as Thomas of the Isles, arrived at the market. He too was very strong, and used to go around the markets challenging others to trials of strength, from which he always emerged victorious. Munro was an ill-natured bully, unlike the gentle Alexander.

After Munro arrived at the market, he was told that Alexander Gunn was a rival to him, and so he set out to issue a challenge. He discovered which tent Alexander was in and that his servant was standing outside the entrance with a silver cane. Munro approached the servant, grabbed the cane, and strode off with it. The servant shouted after him that he wanted it back, but Munro replied: "Let your master come for it!" Munro then stood a fair distance away from the tent waiting for Gunn to emerge.

The servant went for Alexander, who calmly walked up to Munro, and very politely asked for his cane back. Munro held out the cane in both hands and told Alexander that he could have it if he took it from him.

Alexander grabbed the cane and, with a quick jerk, lifted Munro clean off his feet and threw him over his head, landing on his back in the mud. The crowd, which had gathered to see what would happen, laughed loudly at Munro, who picked himself up like a wounded puppy, and shouted: "But for one man, I would clear the whole market stance of every one of you." Munro's dignity was so shattered that he returned to his island home and never visited Caithness again.

Alexander's sister Janet married a Sinclair from Shurrery, Reay. The wedding was a great event for the family and the Clan Gunn in general, and the Clan piper, Hector Gunn, travelled from Baddanloch in East Sutherland for the celebration.

When the wedding party arrived at the church there was another couple waiting to be married, so the minister called both couples in order that he could marry them with one ceremony. Multiple weddings were not uncommon in churches at that time, but there was also the belief that the first bride out of the church had all the best luck for the future.

Whenever the ceremony was over the other bride made a rush for the door, but two of the Clan Gunn caught hold of her and kept her. A general scuffle then ensued, in which some of the guests lost their kilts, but in the end Janet Gunn managed to get out of the door first.

Alexander now mustered the party and called on the piper to play the pibroch *The Gathering of the Clan Gunn for Battle*, and with this tune the piper led them back to the house at Dalnaglaton. They then retired to the barn where the night was passed in feasting and dancing.

A lively dance was in progress when a sergeant and three soldiers of the press gang entered, looking for recruits. Alexander ordered them to leave the dance, but they refused. He then picked up each of the soldiers in turn and threw them out of the barn.

The sergeant then left the building, knowing the treatment that he was going to get, and shouted that Alexander Gunn would not dare behave in such a manner if his master had been there. Alexander asked who his master was, and was told that he was Captain Sutherland of Wester Loch. Alexander said he would treat him in a worse manner than he had treated his servants.

The gang went home with cuts and bruises and complained to the captain about the treatment they had received at the hands of Alexander Gunn. Sutherland vowed that he would kill Gunn with his sword when he met him at Spittal Hill market seven miles south of Thurso. Sutherland was said to be one of the best swordsmen in Scotland at that time and was quite confident that Alexander Gunn would last only a few seconds before his blade.

On the day of the market, Captain Sutherland arrived early and strutted around asking for Alexander Gunn. He was told that he would easily know Alexander when he arrived, as he would be a whole head above the others and he would be wearing a scarlet coat. Captain Sutherland proudly boasted that this would be the last time he would wear it.

As Alexander neared the market, he was told that Sutherland was there seeking revenge. Thus forewarned, he secured an oak cudgel about four feet long and a small stool to act as a shield. With these weapons Alexander approached Sutherland, who cursed him and threatened to make light through his body with his sword.

The fight then started and the sound of blows resounded around Spittal Hill as Alexander parried every move made by the captain's sword with his cudgel. The crowd left the stalls to watch this exciting contest between a renowned swordsman and a hill-man armed with a club. A vicious blow from the captain was expertly parried and Alexander swung his club, breaking the captain's sword into pieces and driving the hilt into his hand.

When Alexander saw that the captain was injured, he quietly inquired if he had enough. The captain turned away in shame and fear, called for his horse and rode off home in disgrace.

A few years later, Alexander was desperately in need of grain as an early frost had blighted all the crops at Dalnaglaton. He heard that Captain Sutherland had some to spare at Mey, so he set off to try and obtain some. On the way they met the captain and a party out shooting. Alexander was afraid that the captain might kill him so asked his servant to remove his plaid, and, if the captain showed any signs of cocking his gun, to throw it over the weapon. The captain approached and shouted:

"Is this you, big Gunn? Are you as good a man as you were at Spittal Market?"

"Yes!" replied Alexander. "If you will lay down your firearm."

The captain then changed his attitude and became very friendly and invited him to his house. He told Alexander: "I well remember when you smashed my sword at Spittal Hill, I was completely at your mercy and your kindness was more than I deserved. I never believed that a man on the face of the earth could do what you did, but I must admit that my strength is like that of a boy compared to yours." Captain Sutherland then treated Alexander to his best wine and filled his sacks with grain, refusing payment. The two became the best of friends after this.

Alexander's brother Donald, who did not possess any great strength, seldom left any market or wedding without becoming involved in a fight. Donald boasted that he caused the fights and Alexander sorted them out.

Alexander became engaged to Janet Gunn of Kildonan, whose renowned beauty was celebrated in a Gaelic song, but before they were married he contracted a fever and died in 1786 at the early age of twenty-eight.

He is buried in Dirlot Cemetery, but his grave is unmarked. Janet Gunn later married William MacKay, farmer, Braelaid, Braemore, and had a large family.

David Marshall, the Backlass Robber

BACKLASS HILL DOMINATES THE LANDSCAPE around the Watten district in Caithness and up until the beginning of the twentieth century it was the site of a market. If we go further back into the history of Watten, the top of the hill was said to be the site of the public gallows where hangings took place. Before the passing of the Education Act of 1872, there was a school on Backlass Hill. Up until fairly recent times the area around the hill was thickly populated and this can be borne out by the number of ruined croft houses which remain.

In the early part of the 17th century, Backlass Hill was the headquarters of a notorious robber named David Marshall. His real name was said to have been Sutherland and he was believed to have been a native of Kildonan, Sutherland-shire. It is not recorded how he came to reside at Backlass and change his name to Marshall, but it is very possible that it was done to evade punishment on some crimes perpetrated in Sutherland-shire.

Marshall, who became known as the Robber of Backlass, was described as being over six feet in height, proportionately built and endowed with extraordinary bodily strength. In the traditional annals of Caithness, Marshall is described as being similar to Robin Hood as he robbed the rich and gave to the poor.

Marshall gathered a number of henchmen around him at his headquarters at Backlass and his activities spread fear and alarm among the rich throughout the whole of Caithness. To the poor he was very kind and was often known to help widows and people who had poor health.

His creed was that the world's goods were very unfairly distributed and a man who was poor was perfectly justified in taking goods from the rich who had more than enough.

Marshall always attended the cattle markets in Caithness dressed in full Highland dress with broadsword and dirk. The small farmers who sold their livestock handed over their money to David Marshall so that he would keep it safe for them. If they had not taken this precaution with their money, they ran the risk of being robbed on their way home by other robbers who were prevalent in Caithness at that time. Marshall always proved faithful to the trust put in him by the small farmers and returned their money without taking a penny for his own use.

The Laird of Pennyland, Watten, had loaned some money to a friend in Inverness and the friend now wished to pay back the money to him. However, the Laird knew that it would be very difficult to carry the money from Inverness to Watten without being robbed on the way. Eventually he decided that he would ask John Tait, one of his tenants, whom he often employed as a messenger, to go to Inverness and collect the money,

John Tait at first hesitated and said that he was willing to do anything for the Laird, but this journey was long and dangerous and if he did not meet with an accident while crossing the rivers and ferries on the road, he was sure to be robbed on his way home by David Marshall or some of his henchmen.

The Laird said that this was nonsense as Marshall would never know that he was carrying money on this journey. He advised Tait not to tell his wife anything about his journey as women are fond of gossiping and not one in a hundred can keep a secret. The Laird gave Tait a pocket pistol to carry with him for protection. He advised Tait to keep it well charged and if any villain should attempt to rob him, he should draw the pistol and shoot him in the stomach. Tait then agreed to go to Inverness for the money. Before he left, the Laird promised him faithfully that if anything should happen to him on the journey, he would look after his wife and family.

John Tait arrived safely in Inverness where he met the Laird's friend, obtained the money and started on the journey back to Watten. He had arrived at the steep mountain pass of the Ord of Caithness when who should he see walking towards him but the dreaded David Marshall with a smile on his face.

"Hello! John is this you?" cried David. "How are you? You have been at Inverness, I understand."

John saw that there would be no point in denying this to Marshall and told him that he had been at Inverness.

Marshall then asked if he had got the money and John told him that he had got the money. He then asked John if anyone had tried to rob him on the journey from Inverness. John told him that no person had tried to rob him. Marshall said that he was glad to hear this and invited John to sit down on the bank beside him and rest.

John accepted Marshall's invitation but felt very uncomfortable. The old road across the Ord at that time ran near the top of a sheer cliff. They were in the middle of this fearful pass and if Marshall felt inclined to take the money and dispose of John, he had little to do but give him a push and he would be thrown over 200 feet into the sea. John felt that he was in a dreadful situation and completely at the mercy of Marshall. He put his hand in his pocket to draw out the pistol, but on second thoughts he drew it out again. Tait knew that Marshall was armed with a sword and a brace of pistols and he was not really a match for Marshall.

"I see, John," said Marshall, "that you would rather have met anyone but me on the Ord, but do not be alarmed my good fellow, I have no intention of taking a farthing of the money from you. You are a decent, trustworthy chap, and although I am a villain myself, I have respect for an honest man. Now, when I think of it, we will be none the worse of a little refreshment."

He drew out of his pocket, a flask of brandy and a small drinking horn. After he had treated himself to a bumper, he filled another for John. "This is not bad stuff," said Marshall, smacking his lips, "I got it from the Laird of Stanergill's cellar."

They chatted together for some time and then they rose to go on their different ways.

"I am on my way to Helmsdale," said Marshall, "and as it is possible that you may meet some of my friends on the road, show them this (handing him a piece of paper with the initials DM written on it) and they will allow you to pass without the least molestation. Oh! by the way," he added, "one of my firelocks is getting rather the worse of the wear. If you please, I will relieve you of the one you have belonging to the Laird, your master, and you may tell him, with my compliments that I will keep it for his sake."

John gave him the pistol feeling very happy to have got off so lightly. He did not meet any of Marshall's friends on his way home to Watten. He went immediately to the Laird's house, delivered the money and astonished him with his account of his meeting with David Marshall at the Ord.

When carrying out some of his daring exploits, Marshall usually had accomplices along with him and with their assistance he broke twice into Keiss Castle and once into Dunbeath Castle. In a second attempt to break into Dunbeath Castle a desperate battle in which firearms were used ensued between the castle retainers and Marshall's gang. One of Marshall's men was killed by a musket shot and it was said that Marshall carried his body on his back from Dunbeath to his home in Dirlot, a distance of about 20 miles. This feat of strength was often talked about in Caithness for a long time after Marshall left the area.

Marshall continued his lawless life of stealing from the rich and giving to the poor. This caused him to be loved by the poor but he was a thorn under the skins of the Lairds. They were always making plans to try and capture him, but he was always able to escape.

Sir William Sinclair of Keiss, who was often the victim of Marshall's raids on his cellars and other property, made a vow that he would capture Marshall either dead or alive. He gathered together twelve of the strongest men on his estate and armed them all. One night they set off for Marshall's residence at Backlass, Watten, and arrived there just as dawn was breaking.

Sir William ordered six men to keep armed guard on the house while he and the other six men broke down the door and rushed in with loaded pistols in their hands. Marshall had just risen from bed and was in the act of combing his long hair when Sir William and his party broke in. Sir William presented a pistol to his chest and told him that if he offered any resistance he would be a dead man.

Marshall made no attempt to escape and allowed his hands to be bound and he was then taken to Wick where he was lodged in jail. There were so many complaints against Marshall that it was thought unnecessary for him to go through a trial. He was kept in jail for a few days and was then taken out, publicly whipped and banished from Caithness.

It is believed that he either returned to his native Sutherland or some other county in the north of Scotland where he resumed his old profession of robbery and theft. He was eventually arrested by the authorities, brought to trial and banished to the plantations abroad.

The Snowstorm

JANET MCALLISTER WASHED THE DISHES and tidied everything in her thatched house in Corrichoich, Braemore. Her husband John sat beside the fire after working all day on his croft. John and Janet were rather excited as their daughter Marion, an only child, would be home for the night from a farm in Braemore where she worked for Donald McCallum. The next day was the blessed Sabbath and Marion stayed Saturday and Sunday night with her parents and then left early on Monday morning to walk back to Braemore, a distance of about two miles. Meanwhile John and Janet, who were both in their fifties, looked forward to the arrival of their daughter which was the highlight of their week.

The month was November and there was a slight covering of snow on the ground but John thought that there was nothing that would trouble Marion as she knew the track between Braemore and Corrichoich like the back of her hand.

Marion was a great favourite with the McCallum family and always sang as she went about her chores in the house and on the outside work on the land. Donald McCallum had a son named Hector, aged about eighteen, who was two years older than Marion. They were good friends and he treated Marion's singing and cheerful nature as part of the scenery on the farm.

On this Saturday night when Marion left to walk to her home in Corrichoich, Hector was a bit worried about her as there was a slight covering of snow and he hoped that it did not turn into a blizzard.

Marion walked lightly along the path towards Corrichoich which she had walked many times before. The light of the moon on the snow illuminated her way and she hummed a tune as she tripped along. Suddenly the moon began to cloud over, the wind began to blow bringing drifting snow with it and Marion became frightened as she realised that she was being caught in a snowstorm on the moors. The wind blew with vehemence from the north bringing heavy drifting snow obscuring her path. She prayed that she would be given strength to reach her parents' house in safety, but as the storm increased she knew that this was very unlikely. Marion pressed on and fell several times in the snow but on each occasion was able to struggle to her feet again and carry on. As time passed and the fury of the storm continued Marion felt the cold and wetness of the snow overcoming her power to think clearly and she was so tired that she could not care whether she lived or died. Finally she fell into the snow and did not have the strength to rise so she just lay there.

Meanwhile in Braemore Hector McCallum had seen the severity of the snowstorm and his immediate thoughts were with Marion whom he knew could not have reached Corrichoich before the start of the storm. He had always respected Marion and her cheerful ways but now he knew that his feelings were much deeper than that and she was the only person whom he loved in the world.

Hector put on heavy clothing and went out to look for Marion, but by this time the wind was blowing with added vehemence driving the powdered snow with such force that it almost choked him as it blew into his nose and mouth. He prayed as never before that he should be given extra strength so that he could find Marion. His strength began to waver and he felt that he must lie down and give way to the storm but thoughts of Marion egged him on to superhuman efforts as he continued his way along the path towards Corrichoich.

At length he bumped into a bundle on the path which was covered over with snow and found to his horror that it was the prostrate body of Marion. He lifted her up but she was limp and it appeared that she was dead. Hector hugged her close trying to put some warmth into her body and after a short time found that she was still breathing. Hector then attempted to carry her towards Corrichoich, but by this time the storm seemed to be abating as the wind had lost its fury and the snow was lighter.

Hector carried Marion along the path and at last she began to recover consciousness and was able to talk to him. Some distance along the path he came upon another bundle covered over with snow and on uncovering it found that it was Marion's father who was completely exhausted and was on his hands and knees unable to go further. At the start of the storm he had come out to look for Marion, but the fury of the storm had overcome him.

The storm was abating and Hector was able to help both Marion and her father to their home in Corrichoich. Marion's mother was so overjoyed to see that they were all safe that it was some time before she could speak to them.

After they all had recovered from their ordeal, John McAllister said that he would conduct family worship as they must give thanks to the Almighty for having been delivered from the jaws of death. He said that he would begin by reading from Corinthians, Chapter 13. He read, "Though I speak with the tongues of men and of angels and have not charity, I am become a sounding brass, or a tingling symbol." As John McAllister continued with his reading the words made a big impression on Hector. Although at first he could not think what the word charity really meant, he remembered that an old preacher had said that the word charity really meant love. Then substituting the word love for charity, John McAllister's reading had new meaning for him. He ended with the words, "And now abideth faith, hope, love, these three but the greatest of them is love." John McAllister then ended with a prayer giving thanks for their deliverance from the storm.

Hector then went outside the house and found that the wind had ceased and it was now a frosty, moonlit night. He decided to walk back to his home in Braemore as his parents would be worried in case he had got lost in the storm.

Bidding good night to Marion, her father and mother he set out for Braemore. The soft snow was piled high on the path and surrounding heather, causing his feet to sink, making walking rather difficult.

The bleak ridge of the Scaraben Hills '…guarding the valley of Braemore'

To the south lay the Scaraben Hills, resplendent in their white coating of snow as if they were guarding the valley of Braemore.

The last words of John McAllister's bible reading kept going through his head, 'and the greatest of these is love'. Hector had never thought much about the meaning of love before, but this night it seemed very different to him. He had always been on friendly terms with Marion as she went about her work on the farm but apart from that he had never thought much about her. Tonight when the blizzard started she was the only person he could think about as he knew that she would not have reached her home in Corrichoich.

When walking along the track towards Corrichoich he had almost been overcome by the force of the blizzard and the choking snow, but within him rose an overpowering force that told him that he must go on and rescue Marion. This gave him superhuman strength and her face was ever before him as he battled through the blizzard until he found her lying on the path, unconscious and covered with snow. As he carried her towards her home, Hector had realised that she was the most important person in the world to him. Her father had then taught him the meaning of love as he read the 13th chapter of Corinthians.

The stillness of the night and the beauty of the moonlight on the snow made Hector think of his grannie and grandfather who had left this worldly scene a number of years ago and now rested in the peaceful burying ground at Braemore. He remembered their kindness to him in their lives and in the stillness of the night he felt that they were near to him and they were urging him to use kindness as his emblem in life.

Before Hector reached his home, he knew that he was deeply in love with Marion. Romance blossomed between them and a few months later they were married.

A Fight at the Market

IN THE LATTER PART OF the 18th century, Neil Macleod, a native of Sutherland, tenanted a farm in Braemore while on the neighbouring estate of Langwell his friend, Alexander Gordon, who was also a native of Sutherland, had the tenancy of a farm. Macleod and Gordon were both said to have stood about six feet in height, proportionately built, and were said to have possessed extraordinary physical strength. They were described as quiet, peace-loving men.

At that time there was a kind of perpetual feud which went on between Caithness men and Sutherland men. For most months of the year this feud lay dormant and it was only when drink was consumed and tempers were aroused that this disagreement came to the surface again. Cattle markets were the favourite place for these fights taking place where the men from the different districts had their fans in the same way that football teams have their fans today. The Lairds also enjoyed these fights and gave their employees and tenants all kinds of backing and in some cases they even supplied them with clubs.

The market at Dunbeath was due to be held in a few weeks time and men from the estate of Swiney, near Lybster, Caithness, were longing for a fight with their adversaries from the county of Sutherland. The Laird of Swiney, Mr Sutherland, was looking forward to this fight as much as his tenants. His tenants told him that they intended to beat the men from Sutherland at the Dunbeath market. Mr Sutherland asked them if he could do anything to help and they said that it would be of great assistance to them if they could get a supply of hazel cudgels to use as weapons against their opponents. The Laird said that he would get them a supply from Inverness and he would send for them immediately so that they would arrive in good time for the market,

On the day of the Dunbeath market, Mr Sutherland, who was accompanied by his tenants, left early for the market. The tenants were all armed with the hazel cudgels which had arrived at Swiney from Inverness, and they were all spoiling for a fight. When they arrived at the market they found to their great disappointment that there were very few men from Sutherland at it. The only two Sutherland men that they could see were Alexander Gordon from Langwell and Neil Macleod from Braemore.

The business of the market which mainly consisted of buying and selling cattle and horses had almost finished when one of the Swiney men was able to pick a quarrel with Alexander Gordon by accusing him of cheating when selling one of his cows. Gordon knew that this was a malicious accusation and vigorously denied it. This was what the Swiney men wanted and they crowded around their champion who had made the accusation against Gordon.

Heated words then turned to blows as the Swiney man hit Gordon with his cudgel. Gordon was hampered as he was caring for his young son who was then about four years of age. When hit by the cudgel Gordon quickly released the boy's hand, caught the cudgel and wrestled it from the Swiney man, dealing him a blow which laid him prostrate at his feet. The Swiney men then rushed at Gordon but several of them received the same fate. Gordon was in danger of being forced into a corner by the Swiney men owing to their superiority of numbers when his friend Neil Macleod came to his aid. He quickly procured a cudgel by snatching one from a Swiney man.

Gordon and Macleod placed themselves back to back and in this formation were able to deal with the rushes of the Swiney men and every blow with their cudgels laid a man unconscious. When the Swiney men saw what their fate was to be they gave up the fight and left for their homes.

More than a dozen of the Swiney men were so badly injured that they had to be carried home to Swiney. The prominent part played in the fight by Neil Macleod was talked of for many years later in the Highlands of Caithness where it was referred to as Neil Macleod's fight.

The Laird of Swiney must have felt very humble as he made his way home to Swiney. He had organised and planned the battle, supplying his army with weapons only to find that the weapons were to be used to destroy his own army. It was said that he was so downcast by the whole affair that shortly afterwards he sold the Swiney estate.

The Secret of Garrywhin

IN THE 15TH CENTURY, A different kind of liquor was being consumed in Caithness. Although it tasted similar to whisky there was something strange about it as it was neither whisky nor rum and there was a taste of heather from it.

Most inns and change houses sold this strange liquor but no person knew where it came from. There were several people in the county who acted as agents for this liquor and it was usually delivered to the inns under cover of darkness. The liquor proved to be very popular and after a few years became one of the prime drinks in Caithness.

Eventually it was learned that a number of years before this a strange man whose name was believed to be Duncan McGill and his son John had arrived in the county. They lived in a house at Garrywhin near a rocky brae near the west end of Loch Wattenon, Ulbster. No person knew where they came from. Some people said that they came from the Western Isles and others Ireland. What they did for a living was very much a mystery as they were very seldom seen beyond the confines of their house during the day. They had no land on which they could grow barley from which they could distil whisky so they could not be making a living from distilling.

Their house was near Loch Wattenon and rumours began to circulate that they had a cave in the rocky brae which they used for distilling purposes. A search was made of the rocky brae but no person could find the entrance to a cave.

Eventually a watch was kept on the rocky brae. Duncan and John McGill were seen entering a cave by a secret entrance. A short time later several people were seen approaching the secret entrance where they were met by Duncan who took them inside. A short time later they emerged carrying small kegs on their backs so at last the source of the heather whisky was found.

The searchers returned to Garrywhin during the day and made a thorough search of the rocky brae but were unable to find the secret entrance to the cave. They then began to question Duncan and John as to how they made their whisky. Duncan and John admitted that the whisky was made from heather but that was as much as they would say. The searchers then went to their homes and tried to distil whisky from heather but had no success.

Infuriated, the searchers returned to Garrywhin and decided that they would force Duncan and John to reveal their secret. Duncan told them that if he revealed the secret of the heather whisky, his son would kill him for having done so, but if they killed his son he would think about revealing the secret. They killed his son and Duncan then said: "Kill me also and as no one else knows our secret it shall die with me." In their anger they also killed Duncan so the secret died with him.

The rocky brae at Garrywhin has been searched over and over again, but no trace of the secret entrance to a cave has ever been found. Strange reports of a large hairy beast having been seen climbing up through the rocks have given rise to the belief that the area is haunted.

Loch Wattenon at Garrywhin. The rocky brae where Duncan McGill had a secret entrance to a cave is in the background.

Recollections of School Days at Badbea

ALEXANDER GUNN, WHO WAS BORN in Badbea, about 1822, being a son of John Gunn, meal miller, recalled some of his school days at Badbea in a series of articles in the *Northern Ensign* in 1880.

There were twelve families in Badbea and thirteen families in Auchincraig in his youth. Badbea and Auchincraig are parts of the Berriedale and Langwell estates. A few years earlier the two communities had combined to build a school as a community of twelve or thirteen families could hardly have been expected to pay the wages of a school teacher. By combining the two communities this made a total of 25 families that had to share the bill.

The school was built by members of the two communities and was situated just on the Auchincraig side of the border with Badbea. The building measured approximately 20 feet by 12 feet and the walls were built of drystone with no mortar in it. The roof was of thatch with a skylight in it for providing light. A fire was situated in the middle of the room and the smoke made its exit through a hole in the roof. Fuel was provided for the fire by each pupil taking a peat with them to the school every day. There was a guard placed on the peat neuk every morning to see that every pupil brought a peat and woe betide any person who failed to take a peat as they were immediately rewarded with several strokes of the strap. One delinquent felt the punishment dealt out to him as being very unfair and vowed that he would never take another peat with him to school. When reading the lesson he expressed his feelings very strongly in Gaelic, but it is doubtful if the teacher understood.

When Gunn attended the school there were about 70 children in the two districts and about 50 of them were of school age, so this made conditions in the small school rather cramped. When the wind blew in the winter it blew right through the walls as there was no mortar in them to stop it. In an attempt to stop the wind the pupils tried packing the crevices with dried moss. This had the effect of blocking some of the wind but when the snow came it blew right through the walls and formed wreaths inside the school. Many of the children would be sitting in the snow in their bare feet.

Gunn compares the school at Auchincraig where he received his first lesson with a school in the Western Isles of Scotland which was described in a speech made in the House of Lords by the Duke of Argyll during a discussion on the Education Act. He said, "About 20 years ago, I went into a school on one of the Western Isles of Scotland. It was not suited to any rules laid down by the Lord President of the Council. It was what we call a drystane bigging with a thatched roof and a mud floor. On going into the school, I found in it a number of children poorly clad, nevertheless with extraordinary expression of intelligence. One of the subjects given to the children was to read a description of how extracted lead ore was treated. The description given said that it was pounded and subjected to a current of running water to free it from extraneous matter. I then thought that it was impossible that a poor child, so poorly clad could have understood the meaning of such a word. I asked him what was the meaning of extraneous. He answered my question by saying, 'Not belonging to itself.' Now my Lords, I put that same question to many highly cultivated people, and nine out of ten, however highly cultivated they may have been, failed to answer that question as clear and concise as that child."

Gunn said that at that time in no other part of the United Kingdom had education reached such a high standard in proportion to their poor circumstances as in the Highlands and Islands of Scotland. The school at Auchincraig was much the same as was to be found in similar districts

Houses at Badbea, 1903

in Scotland. The snow had free access to it in winter and in the summer the bees found the moss-packed walls an inviting place to rear their young. When the young brood began to move about, the school was like a monster bee hive, and many sore stings were inflicted on the legs and thighs of boys as the bees crept up inside their kilts while they were seated on the forms at their lessons. The forms had no backs on them and the writing desks were of the simplest make.

The teacher who gave Gunn his first lesson was a Badbea lad named John Sutherland who was better known as Balaam. Gunn said that in his opinion he did not possess any qualifications which should have classed him as being fit for the position of teacher. Instead of the usual tawse he had a knotted piece of rope about a third of an inch thick and he was not slow at using it. He really ruled by fear and never had the respect of his pupils.

Sutherland was not long as teacher at Auchincraig and was succeeded by John Grant from Rinsary, Berriedale. He was better educated than Sutherland, was of a jolly nature and always on good terms with his pupils. He continued his education after he left Auchincraig and became a minister.

The ruins of Auchincraig, perched precariously on the sloping cliff top.

Distant view of Badbea and the memorial, situated on the coastal fringe

Close up of the memorial at Badbea

The next teacher was a young man by the name of Sutherland from Balnabruich, Dunbeath. He was well-educated and after he left the school at Auchincraig, he also continued his studies and became a minister.

Saturday was a school day but pupils left earlier on Saturday night so that they could study the Shorter Catechism for Bible lessons. There were no holidays from the school during the summer or the winter so the teacher and pupils had to work all the year round without a break.

During the summer a number of the older pupils stayed away from school and sought work at the herding, on farms and the herring fishing. At one time there were fourteen small boats operating from Badbea and Auchincraig. In the winter they returned to the school.

The teacher had free accommodation with the parents of the pupils. It was arranged that he stayed with the parents one week for each pupil.

The last of the teachers was Donald Bain Mackenzie from Houstry, Dunbeath. He was of a mild, gentle disposition and was more respected by the children. When Mackenzie began teaching the days of the school were numbered as the Laird, Donald Horne had decided to evict the tenants from Auchincraig and turn their holdings into green fields as pasture for his sheep and game and this included the land on which the school had been built.

Eviction notices were served on the tenants of Auchincraig and it did not require a strong body of police and magistrates to carry out the orders of Donald Horne. Thirteen tenants and their families left their homes peaceably to be scattered to the four winds of heaven. These evictions took place towards the end of the 1830s. About that time evictions were taking place in Ireland for non-payment of rents, but in the case of the Auchincraig tenants none were in arrears with their rent, yet they were shown no mercy by Donald Horne who valued money more than human life. Eviction notices were not served on the tenants of Badbea as the barren land on which their houses were built was so poor that there was no value in it as pasture for animals. The families were now left without a school and slowly they began leaving to try and obtain work or land in different parts of Scotland or abroad. By the early part of the 20th century Badbea was deserted.

The ruined remains of the crofthouses at Badbea

In 1911 a memorial was erected at Badbea by David Sutherland of Wairapa and Wellington, New Zealand, in memory of his father Alexander Robert Sutherland, born in Badbea 1806 and died in New Zealand 1877, and other residents of Badbea. The memorial was built on the site of John Sutherland's house. He was well-known as a preacher and was always referred to as John Badbea. He also was an uncle of Alexander Robert Sutherland. The names of several of the residents of Badbea are inscribed on plaques on the memorial.

In early life Alexander Gunn left Badbea and went to Glasgow where he had a successful business career, but his roots were in Badbea and Caithness. He was a prolific writer and regularly contributed articles to local papers in Caithness under the pseudonym of 'A Native of Badbea'.

In June, 1897, he had his last holiday in Caithness and was able to visit the graves of his ancestors in the old cemetery at Berriedale. From there he went to Badbea where he felt ill, but recovered and was able to resume his journey by horse carriage to Portgower meal mill where he stayed

The Berriedale Braes

The old cemetery at Berriedale

the night with his cousin. The next day he arranged for a fisherman to take him on a boat trip around the coast of Badbea so that he could see it from the sea.

He then went to stay with a friend in Golspie where he took ill and died on 11th June, 1897, aged 75 years. Gunn's remains were taken to Glasgow where he was buried in Cathcart Cemetery. He was survived by his wife and grown-up family.

The Last Need Fire

ABOUT 1810 A DISEASE BROKE out among cattle in Houstry, Dunbeath. It was said to have been caused by a man taking earth from a fairy hillock thus infuriating the small folk with the result that they took their vengeance out on the cattle.

At first only a few cattle were infected but it seemed to spread rapidly until more than half were infected and several of them died.

A meeting was held in one of the houses and the advice of old Donald, who was skilled in different types of cures for human and animal illnesses, was sought. He advised that owing to the seriousness of the disease a Need Fire should be lit.

The next day orders were issued to all the householders in Houstry that all fires should be extinguished. They then met on an island in the Houstry Burn where, under the guidance of Donald, the fire was to be lit. A supply of peats and wood for the fire was obtained.

Donald told them to drive two logs of wood into the ground and then a cross bar was fitted on top of the logs making the structure look like the framework of a doorway. A large hole was then bored into the middle of the cross bar. Donald then inserted a bar of wood into the hole and asked two men to keep turning this bar as he hoped that the friction would ignite a fire. An important feature of this ritual was that the men who turned the bar of wood had to be dressed in garments of pure wool and did not have tackets in their boots as any type of iron would undo the ritual. The two men worked hard all day and there was no sign of a spark of fire. Eventually they gave up their task and retired for the night.

Possible site of the last Need Fire in the Houstry Burn

General view of Houstry with the hills of Morven, Scaraben and Maiden Pap as a backdrop.

The next day they all gathered again on the island and Donald was of the opinion that one of the householders had failed to extinguish their fire. A search of all the houses was made and it was found that one old woman had left her fire burning. The fire was extinguished and when the fire-starting procedure was gone through again the fire was ignited.

All the cattle in Houstry were then driven through the smoke of the fire on the island and this was said to have cured the cattle disease. The Need Fire lit in 1810 in Houstry was said to be the last Need Fire in Scotland.

Bloodshed at Berriedale

IN THE EARLY PART OF the seventeenth century the estate of Berriedale was owned by Lord Oliphant who was one of the large estate owners in Caithness at the time. He resided at times at Berriedale Castle, but also owned Oldwick Castle and extensive lands in the parish of Wick.

About 1608 he is said to have sold the Berriedale estate to the Earl of Caithness. A Berriedale family by the name of Sutherland took umbrage at Lord Oliphant having sold the estate to the Earl of Caithness so they took every opportunity that they could find to harass the Earl and his servants.

In October, 1608, John Sutherland took matters into his own hands and with several companions who were all armed went to the home of one of the Earl's servants at Rinsary, attacked him in his house and left him severely wounded.

About January, 1609, the Earl of Caithness sent a number of his men to Millery, Berriedale, to seize corn and cattle from the inhabitants as he claimed that they were in debt to him. John Sutherland, Berriedale, seemed to be one step ahead of the Earl this time as he was waiting for the Earl's men to arrive with a number of the Clan Mackay from Strathnaver in Sutherland. John and his Mackay friends attacked the Earl's men, stripped them of all their clothing and sent them back naked to the Earl on a cold January day. The Earl's pride was severely dented by the actions of John Sutherland and his friends. John then rounded up all the cattle and horses belonging to the Earl that were grazing on

Millery and drove them to Strathnaver. Sutherland then took refuge with Hutcheon Mackay, the Chief of the Strathnaver Mackays, as the Earl of Caithness was desperate to capture him.

In December, 1609, Sutherland and the Mackays made another raid on Berriedale, slew several of the Earl's retainers and servants, stole a quantity of goods and drove off a herd of cattle to Strathnaver.

By this time the Earl of Caithness was really infuriated by the actions of John Sutherland and the Mackays so he complained to the Privy Council. John Sutherland and Hutcheon Mackay were summoned to appear before the Privy Council. Hutcheon Mackay appeared before the Privy Council and was fined. John Sutherland failed to appear so he was denounced a rebel and a warrant was issued for his arrest.

John Sutherland was now forced to live in hiding but from time to time he did appear and continued to harass the Earl of Caithness. Eventually he was arrested and handed over to the Earl who imprisoned him in Girnigoe Castle. Hutcheon Mackay intervened on Sutherland's behalf with the Earl. The Earl eventually decided to free Sutherland as he wished to live on friendly terms with the Mackays of Strathnaver.

Excise Men and Smugglers

AT ONE TIME QUITE AN industry was carried on in the hills around Braemore in making whisky or smuggled whisky as the illegal liquor was called. Whisky stills were hidden in the hills around Braemore and the residents were continually trying to outwit the Excisemen or gaugers as they were called. Whisky at that time was said to be the cure for all ills that could fall upon a person.

A crofter named Donald was a well-known whisky smuggler who often had his house and outbuildings searched by the gaugers who were looking for whisky. Donald was always able to outwit them as he always hid his liquor some distance from his croft. One day he was told that one of the gaugers had been searching premises in Dunbeath for the illicit liquor and would be coming to Braemore.

Donald said, "I will save the gentleman the trouble of coming to Braemore as I will go and meet him."

He then yoked his horse to his cart, filled the cart with peats in the middle of which he hid a small whisky keg. He then drove the horse along the road towards Dunbeath. He had only travelled a short distance when he saw the gauger and two companions approach in a pony and trap. The gauger asked Donald where he was going with the load of peats and he told him that he was going to Dunbeath with it.

"You are not going anywhere with your cart until I search it," said the gauger. The gauger and his assistants then began taking the peats off the cart. He then rubbed his hands with glee when he came upon the whisky keg.

"At last I have caught you and instead of you delivering peats to Dunbeath, I will be delivering you to the jail in Wick."

Donald made out that he was very angry and annoyed at being caught with the whisky keg, but the gauger and his two companions were overjoyed. After Donald's fit of temper seemed to have abated, he asked the gauger if he could have one concession before they started on the long journey to Wick, and that was if he could have one dram of his own whisky. After he had made several more derogatory remarks to Donald, showing how delighted he was with his capture, the gauger finally agreed to give him one dram from the keg. He turned the tap and found that the keg only contained sour milk.

The gauger swore at Donald in disgust as once more he had been outwitted by him. He turned his trap and headed back towards Dunbeath leaving Donald to deliver his peats.

A woman who kept a small inn or change house at Berriedale was in the habit of buying smuggled whisky from Braemore for sale in her premises. One day she had just received a keg of the contraband liquor when she saw a gauger and his assistant approach. The keg was in the living-room of her house so she had no way of disposing of it as they were already approaching the door. She pulled some bedclothes from a box bed, set the keg in front of the fire, covered it over with the bedclothes, sat on it and made out that she was very ill.

When the gauger knocked on the door, she shouted to him to come in as she could not come to the door as she was very ill. The gauger came in, sympathised with her for her illness and left without suspecting that she was sitting on illicit liquor.

A man named William who lived at Corrichoich, Braemore was a well-known whisky smuggler. One day he was engaged in distilling in his barn at home when he saw a gauger and two assistants approach. Knowing that he had no time to dispose of the malt and the still, he grabbed an empty whisky keg, hoisted it on his shoulder and ran towards Morven.

The gauger and his assistants immediately gave chase but as William had a good start on them they chased him for about two miles before they began to catch up with him and by this time he was running up the slopes towards Morven. By this time William knew that his wife and family would have had time to dispose of the malt and the still so he stopped running, sat on the keg and allowed the gauger and his assistants to catch up with him. When they found that the keg was empty and that William had outwitted them their anger knew no bounds.

They returned with William to his house, searched it and all outhouses but found nothing as William's wife and family had hidden the malt and all his equipment. The gauger left Corrichoich annoyed and disgusted that he had been outwitted.

The people in Braemore were said to have had a unique way of poaching grouse and pheasants from the Laird. Whenever they wanted a grouse or a pheasant they soaked oats in whisky. They then spread the oats on the feeding ground of the birds. On eating the contaminated oats they quickly became inebriated and began to fall about so they could be caught very easily.

The Leodibest Battle

DUNBEATH STRATH HAS MANY SITES of historical interest. There are a number of cairns, brochs, standing stones as well as the ruins of croft houses from which the inhabitants were driven by a ruthless Laird by the name of Sinclair who considered sheep to be more important than human life.

A short distance west of the ruined shepherd's cottage at Leodibest, three stones are situated on the north side of the road. The stones measure about two feet in height, are about three feet apart and face north and south. The local people always treated this site as being sacred as it was believed to be the burial place of a high-ranking Viking officer who was killed in a battle near there when Caithness was ruled by the Vikings.

If we look back through the pages of history we will discover that in the early part of the tenth century Caithness was ruled by the Vikings. Caithness and Orkney were ruled by Earl Liotus who held the title of Earl of Orkney and Caithness. Liotus had a brother named Stulius who disputed Liotus's claim to the Earldom.

Stulius travelled to the south of Scotland where he had an audience with the King of Scotland where he aired his grievances. The King decided to give the title of Earl of Orkney to Stulius although Liotus had been installed in the Earldom some years previously.

Stulius returned to Caithness where he gathered a large number of troops which he then transported to Orkney as he knew that his brother was residing there. In Orkney Stulius was able to recruit more troops, but by this time Liotus already had a large army. Liotus attempted to make peace with his brother but Stulius would not agree to peace and at length the two armies met and a bloody battle was fought. In the end Stulius's army was overcome and he had to flee to Caithness for safety.

Liotus then moved from Orkney to Caithness with his army as he feared that his brother Stulius would make another attempt to capture the Earldom.

Stulius is believed to have travelled again to the south of Scotland where he had another audience with the King of the Scots. It is believed that the King gave him some troops to help in his effort to capture the Earldom from his brother.

Stulius is then believed to have travelled north to Sutherland where he had an audience with Comus Magbradus, who was believed to have been a Thane of Sutherland, although he is often referred to in history as being a Scots nobleman. He assembled a large number of Sutherland men which he joined with the Scottish army led by Stulius. Magbradus and Stulius marched at the head of this massive army which they believed to be invincible.

They entered Caithness by Braemore and Stulius's army was much superior in numbers to Liotus's army which was advancing to meet them. The two armies met on mossy ground at a place called Achistiabist, which is now called Leodibest. Although Earl Liotus's army was greatly outnumbered by the opposing army, he had great faith in the fighting ability of his men. He ordered them to keep close together and in this way they would be able to withstand the charge of the larger army.

Stulius's army charged Liotus's army but they were able to withstand the charge. In the heat of battle the strength of the Scots began to abate and some of them began to fall back in disorder. Some time later panic seemed to have gripped the Scots army and they began to flee. When Stulius saw this happen he exerted himself to get his men to follow behind him. He threatened them and by showing a good example by his courage, the Scots began to rally behind him again. The battle turned bitter again which was mainly due to Stulius's leadership, but a short time later he received a fatal blow from a sword and was killed. When his men saw that he had fallen thay gave up the fight and fled.

Liotus had gained the victory but at a heavy price as he was badly wounded and died a few days later. His body was interred at Leodibest where his grave can still be seen. The rest of the slain from the battle were interred at Tout-na-goul which is about half-of-a-mile west of Liotus's grave. There is a cemetery at Tout-na-goul which is still used for burials. Tout-na-goul is said to denote 'The Burial Place of Strangers'.

Over the years writers have confused Toft-in-gall, which is near Spittal, with Tout-na-goul.

Liotus's brother Ludovick succeeded him in the Earldom of Caithness and Orkney.

Swein Asleifson
A Northern Pirate

Courage and Treachery in a 12th Century Viking Adventure

In the 12th century the counties of Caithness, Orkney and Shetland were in the possession of the Norseman and were controlled by two Earls. The Earls ruled with iron rods forcing the natives into submission, but early in the 12th century there lived a man in the Earldom who was more powerful than the Earls themselves. He disposed of Earls and their followers as he wished and his power spread as far as the Isle of Man, Wales and Ireland. He was Swein Asleifson, son of Olaf and Asleif, who was born at Duncansby in Caithness and his father was one of the Norse Governors of Caithness. Swein had at least two brothers, Valthiof and Gunni and records indicate that he had two sons named Olaf and Andres. Andres had a son named Gunni from whom the Clan Gunn is believed to be descended. When Swein was at the height of his power he possessed two strongholds: one at Freswick in Caithness which was known as Lambaborg Castle, and the other a mansion house and drinking hall on the Island of Gairsay on Orkney. The name of Lambaborg Castle was changed to Bucholie Castle and its ruins still stand on a rocky promontory overlooking Freswick Bay. The ruins of his mansion house can be seen on the Island of Gairsay.

When Swein's brother Valthiof was still a youth, he showed great promise as a leader of men and was made governor of the Island of Stroma. At that time Caithness, Orkney and Shetland were ruled by Earl Rognvald and Earl Paul. There was fierce enmity between the two men over the amount of land that each should possess. In their latest encounter Earl Paul had been victorious and he held sway in Orkney while Earl Rognvald resided in Shetland.

A Double Tragedy

Earl Paul organised a great Yuletide feast at Orphir in Orkney and invited many guests, among them Valthiof from Stroma. Valthiof set out for Orphir with ten men in a boat, but on the way a terrible storm overtook them and they were all drowned. At the same time, Olaf organised a large feast at Duncansby to celebrate Yule: among his guests were to be his two sons Swein and Gunni, and Swein's friends Asbiorn and Margad from Swona. Three nights before Yule Swein, Asbiorn and Margad went out fishing while Asleif and Gunni went to visit friends. The night after they left, Olivir Rosta, a grandson of Frakork who was one of Olaf's greatest enemies, surprised Olaf in his house. After he had plundered the house he set it on fire, burning Olaf and five of his retainers. The rest of the retainers were allowed to escape.

Swein and his party returned on Yule Eve to find his father's house burned down and to be told that his father had perished in the flames. Afterwards Swein took his mother's name and at first was known as

Gairsay today

Swein, Asleif's son, and later as Swein Asleifson. He immediately went over to Orphir to Earl Paul and invited him to join in the celebration of Yule. At that time, Swein was unaware that his brother Valthiof had been drowned.

At the feast Swein Asleifson was placed on one side of Earl Paul and on the other side sat Swein Briostreif, one of Paul's henchmen, who had served him well in battle. After the feast was over a dispute arose between Swein Asleifson and Swein Briostreif over the amount of drink that each had been given by Earl Paul. Swein Briostreif threatened to kill Swein Asleifson, but Swein Asleifson hid in the shadows of the banqueting hall and killed Swein Briostreif as he passed with a blow from his battle axe. Swein Asleifson escaped by jumping out of a window; Swein went to Egilsey to Bishop William and confessed to having killed Swein Briostreif whereupon the Bishop thanked him for ridding the Islands of such a wicked man, and he hid Swein until Yuletide had passed. Swein then escaped to the Hebrides where he stayed with Holbodi Hundison in Tiree. Holbodi was a great Norwegian chief and received Swein with much hospitality.

Early in the spring Swein left Tiree and went to Athole where he stayed with Earl Maddad and Margaret, Hakon's daughter, who was a sister of Earl Paul. Margaret was a very wicked person and while Swein was with her, they discussed a plan whereby Swein was to capture Earl Paul and take him to Athole where she would force him to hand over his share of the Earldom to her son Harald, who would then be installed as Earl. However, Swein heard of disturbances in the Orkneys and decided to return home accompanied by a nobleman named Liotolf. They first went to Thurso where they visited Ottar, a brother of Frakork. Liotolf was keen to make peace between Swein and Ottar who also wanted to compensate Swein for the damage done by his sister Frakork. In return Swein pledged his friendship to Ottar.

Earl Paul's demise

Swein changed his ship at Thurso and took a barge with a crew of thirty. He then crossed over to Rousay in Orkney. At one end of the island there is a headland and beneath it a large heap of stones which was a favourite resort of otters. As Swein's boat was being rowed towards the island, he saw men among the pile of stones. He ordered twenty of his men to hide in their hammocks while ten men rowed so that they could get close to the island and ask for news. When they came close to the headland the men on shore mistook them for merchantmen and told them to go to Westness where they could bring their cargo ashore for Earl Paul. They were told that Earl Paul was living at Westness and had now gone to hunt otters at the pile of stones. Swein, who was hiding in his hammock, told his men to land where they could not be seen from the headland. They landed and crept up on Earl Paul and his party. A fierce fight ensued and in the end Earl Paul was taken prisoner and nineteen of his party were killed. Six of Swein's men were killed in the engagement.

Swein put Earl Paul on board his ship and sailed to the mouth of the River Oykell near Dornoch in Sutherland. Leaving his ship there, Swein and his party journeyed overland with Paul still captive until they came to Earl Maddad and Margaret at Athole. Earl Maddad received them well and put Paul in his high seat. Margaret then entered with her train of ladies and advanced towards her brother, but he did not appear to be amused. Entertainment was staged for Paul but he was too preoccupied with his worries to enjoy himself.

One day while Swein, Margaret and Paul were together, Margaret said to Swein that he should return to the Orkneys to ask Earl Rognvald if he wished to share the islands with Earl Paul or her son Harald. However, Paul decided that due to his capture and abduction from the islands – in a manner most unfitting and shameful for an earl – he did not want to return to the Orkneys again and he gave his share to Harald. He asked Swein to tell his friends that he had been blinded and maimed so that they would not ask him to go back to the Orkneys.

This is the way Swein related the story of what had happened to Earl Paul, but there is a different version of what may have occurred. This suggests that Margaret induced Swein to blind her brother. She then threw him into a dungeon and had him put to death. We do not know which of the stories is true, but Earl Paul never returned to the Orkneys and seems to have disappeared from history. Swein returned to the Orkneys where all the people were mystified by the sudden disappearance of Earl Paul. He went first to Bishop William and confessed what he had done to Earl Paul. The Bishop asked Earl Rognvald to grant security to Swein and he agreed.

Earl Rognvald was holding a Yule feast at Scapa when Bishop Jon from Athole arrived to see him. Bishop Jon was given a gracious welcome and then went to Egilsey where he met Bishop William. The two bishops returned to Scapa and told Earl Rognvald of the agreement between Earl Maddad and Swein, that Maddad's son Harald should share the Orkneys with Rognvald. An agreement was finally reached between the two Bishops, Earl Rognvald and Swein.

In due course, when Harald went to the islands he was accompanied by Thorbiorn Klerk who was a wise, great man. Harald was very young and Thorbiorn was given the title of foster father and managed Harald's lands. While in the Orkneys, Thorbiorn married Swein's sister Ingrid. Meanwhile Swein had taken possession of all the estates belonging to his father Olaf, and his late brother Valthiof. He became a great chief and always had many men around him. Swein and Thorbiorn were said to be the most powerful men in the North of Scotland and they were great friends.

Swein's vengeance

Shortly afterwards Swein asked Earl Rognvald for ships and men so that he might take vengeance on Frakork and her nephew Olivir Rosta for the burning of his father Olaf. At first Earl Rognvald tried to dissuade Swein from going on such a mission, but Swein persisted and in the end was given two ships with men.

Frakork and Olivir were at that time residing in a house at Kildonan in Sutherland. They constantly feared that an attack would be made from the coast, around the Helmsdale area and the coast was always kept guarded. When Swein's ships were ready he sailed to Duffus in Morayshire and then went to Athole to visit Earl Maddad. He returned from Athole and sailed to the mouth of the River Oykell, near Dornoch. Swein and his party walked overland to Strath Helmsdale because Frakork and Olivir would not expect an attack to come from this direction. The party were on a slope behind Frakork's house before they were spotted. Olivir rallied sixty of his men and attacked Swein. Swein's men fought bravely and Olivir's men were forced to retreat towards the house and a number of them were killed. When Olivir saw that his men were defeated he ran from the ranks towards Helmsdale River and made his escape to the mountains and then to the Hebrides. Swein plundered the house and set it on fire burning Frakork and all the inmates – the same cruel death that she inflicted on Swein's father. Swein and his men then raided several places in Sutherland before returning to their ships.

Swein went on a viking raid plundering several places throughout Scotland. At that time it was considered an honourable occupation for the Norsemen to go on pirate raids throughout the summer. In the autumn Swein returned to the Orkneys laden with booty and visited Earl Rognvald. He then crossed to Caithness where he spent the winter in Lambaborg Castle.

Hold and Holbodi

Shortly afterwards he received a message from Holbodi in the Hebrides asking him to come to his aid as Hold from Wales had attacked him, driven him from his estates and taken much booty. When Swein received the message, he went to the Orkneys and asked his friend Earl Rognvald for ships and men so that he could go to the aid of his friend Holbodi. The Earl gave Swein two ships fully manned, but warned him before leaving to be very careful as the men from the Hebrides were very treacherous. Swein sailed to the Hebrides but could find no trace of Holbodi and was informed that he had fled to the Isle of Man. He therefore sailed to the Isle of Man where Holbodi was glad to see him. Hold had plundered the Isle of Man and killed many men including a nobleman named Andrew, who left a widow, Ingrid, and a son Sigurd. Andrew was one of the wealthiest men in the Isle of Man and all his estates had fallen to his widow. Holbodi advised Swein to woo Ingrid, which he did, and after a short time he proposed marriage to her. She

Lambaborg as it is today

accepted his proposal but made it a condition that he should try to avenge the death of her husband. Swein promised that he would do his best to try and kill Hold.

Swein and Holbodi mounted an expedition with five ships. They plundered Wales and committed many ravages there, but Swein did not come face to face with Hold. Hold knew that Swein was after him so he fled to the Island of Lundy in the Bristol Channel. This island was well fortified and although Swein beseiged it for some time, he was unable to take it and capture Hold. In the autumn Swein and Holbodi were forced to return to the Isle of Man.

The Stacks of Duncansby

Holbodi returned to the Hebrides and in the winter Swein married Ingrid. The couple lived in the Isle of Man where Swein was greatly honoured by the inhabitants. The next spring Swein gathered his men together and went to the Hebrides to seek assistance from Holbodi as he still wished to settle matters with Hold. Holbodi excused himself from helping Swein saying that many of his men were working on the land while others were in sailing ships. The truth was that Holbodi had secretly made peace with Hold, but he did not wish Swein to know this as he would call him a coward. Swein set sail with three ships on pirate raids, but made very little booty during the early part of the summer. He later seized and plundered a barge belonging to monks from the Scilly Isles. He also made several raids on Ireland and in the autumn returned with great spoils to the Isle of Man.

Swein was not long in the Isle of Man when he heard of Holbodi's treachery, although at first he did not believe it. One night in the spring Swein was informed that enemies were approaching his house. Arming themselves, Swein and his men ran out and saw a number of men carrying fire towards his house. Swein and his followers took up their position on the top of a hill and defended themselves against the attackers. A warning horn was sounded by Swein and soon all the inhabitants of the district flocked to his aid. The attackers were soon beaten back towards their ships and many were killed on the way. Leader of the attack was Holbodi who managed to escape in a ship. He went to Lundy Island where he was welcomed by his friend Hold. After this Swein kept a large guard on his house as he distrusted the men from the Hebrides.

Before the next spring Swein left his lands in the Isle of Man and went on a viking voyage to the Island of Lewis where he committed many ravages. He then returned to Gairsay in Orkney to his farm and house. Earl Rognvald visited Swein shortly after his return.

It soon became known to Swein that Holbodi had returned to the Hebrides. He procured five ships from Earl Rognvald so that he could seek revenge on Holbodi. Thorbiorn Klerk was the commander of one of the ships; Halfidi commanded the second; Dufnial the third; Rikyard commanded the fourth ship and Swein himself took the fifth. The ships sailed towards the Hebrides, but when Holbodi learnt that Swein was on his way he fled and never visited the Hebrides again. Swein and his companions ravaged and looted the Hebrides killing many people and they took a large amount of booty. Swein wished to remain in the Hebrides during the winter but Thorbiorn Klerk and the other ships' commanders wanted to return to the Orkneys. In the autumn they returned to Duncansby in Caithness where they were to divide their booty. Swein said that he should have a chief's share as it was he who had the quarrel with the men from the Hebrides. All the commanders asked for an equal share of the booty, but they finally had to submit to Swein as all his men were with him at Duncansby.

Thorbiorn went to the Orkneys and told Earl Rognvald that Swein had deprived them of some of the spoil. The Earl said that this was not the first time that Swein had failed to share his spoils equally, but rather than make an enemy of Swein, he paid them money to compensate for Swein's cheating. Thorbiorn replied

"May God reward you, my Lord, for the honour you do us, and we shall not quarrel with Swein about this, but I shall never be his friend any more, and I shall do him respite in return."

Shortly afterwards by means of revenge, Thorbiorn divorced himself from Swein's sister Ingrid, and sent her to Swein in Caithness. Swein gave his sister a great welcome, but considered Thorbiorn's conduct a terrible insult and after this there was fierce enmity between them.

Margad and Swein alienate Earl Rognvald

While Swein was in the Hebrides he left Margad, Grim's son, in charge of his estates in Caithness and transferred to him the office of Deputy or Factor which he held from Earl Rognvald. Margad treated the people roughly and became very unpopular because of his violence. The people complained about Margad's conduct to Hroald in Wick. Shortly afterwards Margad went to Wick with nineteen men, attacked Hroald's residence and killed him along with several of his followers. Margad confided in Swein when he returned from the Hebrides. They both expected reprisals from their enemies so they went to Lambaborg Castle where they could fortify themselves. Swein and Margad then committed many robberies in Caithness and brought their spoils back to Lambaborg Castle. The people of Caithness were enraged by their conduct and complained to Earl Rognvald.

Hroald's son, also named Swein, asked the Earl that he should have redress against Margad and Swein for the death of his father. He was supported in his cause by Thorbiorn, Halfidi and Dufnial whom Swein had cheated. They pressed the Earl to take severe measures against Swein and Margad. Earl Rognvald, accompanied by these chiefs and a strong body of men, crossed over to Duncansby in Caithness only to find that Swein and Margad were not there. They were told that Swein had moved to

The siege at Lambaborg

Lambaborg Castle. When Earl Rognvald and his men reached Lambaborg Castle, Swein asked who was the leader of the party. He was told that it was Earl Rognvald and he then asked what the Earl wanted. Swein was told to deliver Margad to the Earl. Swein asked if Margad was to receive any mercy, but the Earl said that he would not make any promises.

Swein replied:

"I have not the heart to deliver Margad into the power of Swein, Hroald's son, or my other enemies who are with you, but I should wish very much to be at peace with you, my Lord."

Then Thorbiorn Klerk said:

"Hear what the traitor says, that he would willingly be at peace with his Lord after he has plundered his land and betaken himself to the highways like a thief. You make a bad return to the Earl for all the honour he has done to you, and so you will do to all you can."

Swein's escape from Lambaborg

Swein replied:

"You need not say much in this case, Thorbiorn, for no respect will be paid to your words. But it is my foreboding that you will repay him worse for all the honour he has done to you before you part, for nobody will gain good fortune from any dealings with you."

Then Earl Rognvald intervened and said that the two men should not shout at each other. Earl Rognvald and his men attacked the castle but were unable to take it. They did cut off all supplies to the castle and decided to camp in the vicinity until the defenders were starved out. When the provisions in the castle were almost exhausted Swein called his men together and consulted them. They all said that they wished to stay with Swein as long as they were able.

Swein then said:

"I think it is disgraceful to starve here and afterwards to surrender to our enemies. It has turned out, as was likely, that our skill and good fortune should fail against Earl Rognvald. We tried to secure peace and security for life, but neither was to be for my companion Margad. Though I know that the others will be able to obtain quarter, yet I have not the heart to deliver him under the axe. Still it is not right that so many here should suffer for his difficulties, although I am unwilling to part from him for a time."

Swein and Margad make their escape

A plan was resolved and Swein tied together ropes reaching from the castle down to the sea, a distance of over 150 feet. During the night Swein and Margad were lowered into the sea and they swam alongside the rocks until they came to a beach where they were able to get ashore. They walked overland to Sutherland where they considered themselves to be safe from Earl Rognvald and his men. After Swein and Margad had been given time to get safely away, the defenders of the castle surrendered to Earl Rognvald and were shown mercy.

From Sutherland, Swein and Margad journeyed until they came to Duffus in Morayshire where they met some Orkneymen in a trading vessel. Halyard and Thorkel were the commanders. Swein and Margad joined them bringing their numbers up to twelve. They sailed south to the Isle of May where there was a monastery. Swein and his men had to stay there for seven nights because of the weather. They told the monks that they had been sent by Earl Rognvald to the King of the Scots. Suspecting their story and thinking that they were pirates the monks sent to the mainland for men to defend the monastery. When Swein and his companions knew this had happened, they plundered the monastery and sailed away. They journeyed to the Firth of Forth and then visited David, King of the Scots, in Edinburgh. Swein was well received by King David and he stayed with him for some time. King David sent his men to all those who had been robbed by Swein, and told them to estimate their losses so that he could make compensation.

King David asked Swein to bring his wife from Orkney and he would give him any honours in Scotland that he wished, or grant any request that he might make. Swein said that he would like Margad to stay with him, and that the King should send a message to Earl Rognvald asking the Earl to be reconciled to Swein, but he would leave the decision entirely to Earl Rognvald. Swein added that he was happy when on friendly terms with the Earl, but ill at ease when at war with him.

King David replied:

"I suppose this Earl is a good man and you value nothing except what comes from him, since you prefer the risk of surrendering yourself to his good faith, and refuse my offers."

King David intervenes

Swein said that he would never give up his friendship with the King, but he asked that the King should use his powers to facilitate a reconciliation between him and Earl Rognvald. King David granted Swein his request. Men were sent to the Orkneys with presents for Earl Rognvald and a message requesting that the Earl should make peace with Swein. Swein also went north to the Orkneys, while Margad remained in Edinburgh with the King. King David's messengers were well received by Earl Rognvald and he became fully reconciled to Swein who now returned to his estates.

Some time later Earl Rognvald went on a pilgrimage to Jerusalem and while he was away Erlend went to King Malcolm and requested that he should be given the title of Earl and should share Caithness with Earl Harald. King Malcolm (David's grandson and successor) granted him this request. Bitterness existed between Harald and Erlend for some time but eventually a truce was signed.

A lengthy feud with Harald

Swein was living at Lambaborg Castle with his son Olaf by his first wife Raghhild (Ingimund's daughter). His second wife was Ingrid (Thorkel's daughter) and their son was named Andres. Earl Harald was living in Wick at the time. Swein saw a transport vessel coming from the north through the Pentland Firth. He knew it was one of Harald's ships, carrying his rents from Shetland. He ordered his men to capture the vessel and he had Harald's crew put ashore at Freswick and ordered them to walk to Wick. When the crew reached Wick and told Earl Harald what had happened, he was furious and said:

"Swein and I shall have our turns."

Shortly afterwards Swein went with two boats to the Orkneys where he captured a ship which was carrying a valuable cargo from Lewis to Earl Harald. He also stole twelve ounces of gold from the house of Sigurd Klaufi, a friend of Harald.

Swein then returned to Caithness and sailed on to Aberdeen where he visited King Malcolm. He was very hospitably entertained by the King and spent some time with him. Swein was such a powerful man at that time that King Malcolm did everything in his power to remain friends with him. After his meeting with the King, Swein returned to the Orkneys. Upon his return, a meeting was arranged between Swein and Earl Erlend who was then his bitter enemy. They negotiated for a whole day and finally a truce was made between them. Earl Erlend had just returned from a visit to the King of Norway who said that he should have the part of the Orkneys which was held by Earl Harald. Swein suggested they should go to Earl Harald and ask him to give up the land in Orkney. They sailed in search of Harald and saw him on board his ship at Careston, near Stromness. When Earl Harald saw long ships approaching he expected trouble, so he and his men left their ship and went into a nearby castle. Earl Erlend and Swein attacked the castle with arms and fire, but Harald and his men defended it bravely and by nightfall there were many dead on both sides. Erlend and Swein were forced to abandon the attack and retire to their ships.

The next morning The Boendr (a Viking official) and some friends arrived and tried to make peace between the two Earls. Earl Erlend and Swein were very reluctant but in the end they agreed, on condition that Harald gave Erlend his share of the Orkneys. Earl Harald agreed to this and returned to Caithness with the few of his men still alive.

Earl Erlend, Swein and The Boendr then went to Kirkwall where Erlend was installed as Earl. When Yule was approaching Swein went home to his estate at Gairsay and left Erlend, but before leaving, he warned Erlend to be on his guard for an attack from Harald and the Scots. On the eleventh day of Yule it happened in Gairsay that Swein was sitting at his drink with his men when suddenly he began rubbing his nose and announced:

"I think Earl Harald is now on his way to the Islands."

His men said that they thought this was very unlikely as there was a strong gale at the time. Swein replied:

"I know such is your opinion and I shall therefore not send intelligence to the Earl now, merely on the strength of my presentiment, yet I suspect it is necessary."

Earl Harald had started his journey to the Orkneys during Yuletide, with four ships and one hundred men. For two nights they lay under Grimsey and then landed at Orphir where they left their ships. They then walked to Firth and spent the Yule holiday near Maeshowe where two of their men were seized with madness owing to the amount of drink consumed. They were told that Earl Erlend was on board his ship in Firth, but during the day had been drinking at a house ashore. Harald and his party attacked this house, killing one of the occupants and taking four prisoners. At the time of the attack, Earl Erlend was safely on board his ship. Harald then returned to Thurso taking his prisoners with him. When Erlend learnt of Harald's presence, he immediately sent a messenger to Swein who joined Erlend with his fleet of boats, staying with him for the rest of the winter.

Swein and Earl Erlend decided to go raiding and they sailed into the Moray Firth and along the east coast of Scotland until they came to Berwick on Tweed where there lived a wealthy merchant by the name of Knut. Swein seized one of Knut's vessels which was bound for Berwick with a valuable cargo. Knut's wife was also on board. Swein then continued south to the Fern Islands. When Knut heard that his ship and his wife had been taken by Swein, he gathered together as many men as he could find. He gave each man one hundred marks of silver and told them to try and recover his ship and his wife.

Fourteen ships from Berwick put to sea in search of Swein. When Swein saw the fleet from Berwick approaching the Fern Islands he ordered his ships to sail out to sea and thus avoided a conflict. We are not told what became of Knut's wife.

After being at sea for some time Swein put into the Island of May and then sent men to Edinburgh to tell the King of the Scots about his plunder. On their way to Edinburgh, Swein's party met twelve men on horseback who had saddlebags filled with silver. The horsemen enquired after Swein. They said that the King of the Scots had heard that he had been taken prisoner by the men from Berwick and they were on their way to ransom him. The King received Swein's messengers well and sent him a costly shield and other presents. He did not appear to have any sympathy for Knut's loss.

Swein and Earl Erlend arrived back in the Orkneys in the late autumn loaded with plunder. Earl Rognvald also returned to the Orkneys before Yule, from his pilgrimage to the Holy Land. A conference was held at Kirkwall between Rognvald and Erlend to try and make peace between them. The agreement reached was that they should each have half of the Orkneys Islands, and both should defend them against Earl Harald. However, a meeting was subsequently arranged between Earl Harald and Earl Rognvald and a truce was agreed. They decided to go that night and attack Erlend who was living in South Ronaldsay. Swein was with Earl Erlend in South Ronaldsay and when the two Earls landed with large forces, Swein and Erlend sailed over to Caithness leaving word that they intended to escape to the Hebrides. Swein and Earl Erlend then made raids into the interior of Caithness and drove off large herds of cattle and took them on board their ships at Thurso. Swein sent a man over to Orkney to inform Earl Rognvald that he intended to go to the Hebrides. When Earl Rognvald heard this, he called his men together and said:

"For now Swein may be expected every hour in the Islands: the more certainly, the more he talks of going away."

Early in the winter Swein and Earl Erlend left Thurso and sailed by the west coast of Scotland. They had six large ships all well manned, but as the weather was very rough, they had to row. When Earl Rognvald learned of this, he relaxed his watches and brought his ships to Scapa.

Upon reaching Assynt in west Sutherland, Swein and Erlend ordered that the ships should turn around and set their sails. There was a fine breeze blowing and the ships sped towards Hoy in Orkney. When Swein reached Hoy he was informed that the two Earls were in Scapa with thirteen ships. Swein decided to attack the Earls during the night as he thought that this would be in his favour because his men were outnumbered by more than two to one. Earl Rognvald had left his ship and gone ashore to visit friends on the night that Swein attacked. Earl Harald and his men were taken completely by surprise and suspected nothing until they heard Swein's battle cry. Harald and his men defended themselves bravely, but were overcome by the ferocity of Swein's attack. Earl Harald ran ashore and escaped when only five men were left alive in his ship. When the remainder of his men in the other ships saw that their leader had fled, they followed suit by trying to run or scramble ashore. Many of them were cut down by the battle axes of Swein's men, but some of them did succeed. Over one hundred of Earl Harald's men were killed and several were wounded. Four of Swein's men were killed and he took all thirteen ships belonging to the two Earls with all the valuables they contained. Swein then went in search of Earl Rognvald but with no success. The Earl had escaped to his residence at Orphir where he found Earl Harald already hiding. Subsequently, they escaped to Caithness.

Earl Erlend and Swein shared out the valuables from the captured ships. Swein took as part of his share all the treasures that were in Earl Rognvald's ship and later returned them to the Earl in Caithness. Swein advised Erlend to move the ships to Walls where they could see ships coming in from Caithness, but Erlend was persuaded by his men to go north to Damsey where there was a large castle. They drank all day in the castle and at night they fastened the ships together and slept on board.

Erlend perishes

Swein left them and went to Sandwick to visit his kinswoman Singrid to settle a dispute between her and a neighbour. While at Sandwick he heard that Erlend was not taking his advice and not sleeping on board his ship. Swein sent his friend Margad and two other men to the Earl and told him to heed his advice. Earl Erlend said that he would pay attention to Swein's advice and sleep on board his ship at night. That particular night Erlend and twenty-four men went on board one of the ships, but the rest of the men paid no attention to Swein's warning and slept ashore. Earl Erlend continued to drink after he went on board the ship and retired for the night dead drunk. That very night Earl Rognvald and Earl Harald attacked Earl Erlend and none of the watchmen saw them until they were boarding the ships. One of Earl Erlend's men, named Ufi, tried to rouse him but was unable to do so, due to his drunken state. He took Erlend in his arms and jumped overboard into a small boat which was moored alongside the ship, but was unable to get any further and Erlend was slain by one of Harald's men. Most of the other men on board the ship were also slain. Earl Erlend's body must have floated away in the sea as it could not be found after the battle. Earl Harald wished to make peace with Erlend's men who were on shore, but Earl Rognvald asked him to wait to see if Earl Erlend's body could be found. Two nights before Yule a spear was seen sticking in a pile of seaweed on the shore and on closer inspection it was found that the spear was fast in Earl Erlend's body, covered with the seaweed. The body was brought to the church and peace given to the remainder of Earl Erlend's men.

After Earl Erlend's death Swein went to Rendale where he met Margad who gave him the details of how Erlend was killed. Swein and his men then sailed to Rousay where they brought all the tackle from their ships on shore and hid it. They then hid themselves at a homestead where three of Earl Harald's men were staying. The men were Thorfinn, his son Ogmund and Thorfinn's brother-in-law Erlend. Thorfinn and his companions were unaware that Swein and his men were at the house, and during the night Erlend was boasting to his friends how he had given

Earl Erlend the death blow. Swein overheard this boast and immediately rushed in and killed Erlend with his battle axe. Thorfinn was taken prisoner and his son Ogmund was badly wounded.

Harald and Swein – a short-lived peace

Soon after, Swein received a message from Earl Rognvald inviting him to spend Yule with him at Damsey and Swein accepted. Earl Rognvald arranged a meeting for Swein and Earl Harald to try and make peace between them. Harald and Swein bargained for some time and eventually a pact was reached. The final agreement was that Swein should pay a mark of gold to each of the Earls and he should keep half of his estates and one long ship. When Swein agreed to this, he said the agreement would only remain good if he was not oppressed. Earl Rognvald would not accept any payment from Swein, saying that he considered his friendship worth more than money.

Shortly after this truce, Earl Harald went to Gairsay and wasted Swein's corn and other crops. Swein complained of his loss to Earl Rognvald and said that this was a breach of their agreement. He told the Earl that he intended to go home and look after his property but Earl Rognvald advised him not to go as he would be greatly outnumbered by Harald's men. Swein was determined to get even with Earl Harald so he went to Gairsay in a boat with ten men, arriving late in the evening. At first Swein decided to burn down his house and drinking hall, thinking that Harald was inside. However, one of Swein's companions dissuaded him as they did not know if Earl Harald was inside, and if it was set alight Swein's wife and daughter would be burned.

Swein and his men entered the house and found several of the Earl's men, but Harald was not there. When they saw Swein, Earl Harald's men immediately surrendered and gave up their weapons. Swein gave quarter to all of the men. He then poured out all the beer that was in his drinking hall and took his wife and daughter with him for their safety. He returned some weapons to Harald's men before leaving Gairsay.

Earl Harald had gone to Hoy to hunt hares and his men went and told him what Swein had done. Meanwhile, Swein sailed to Eller Holm.

Harald immediately launched a boat and sailed to Eller Holm to settle matters once and for all with Swein.

Swein was out in a small boat near Eller Holm when he saw Harald's ship approach. He knew that Harald's ship would soon overtake him so he devised a devious plan of escape. On one side of Eller Holm there were high rocks and a cave, the mouth of which flooded at high water. It was ebb tide when Swein approached the cave so he sailed right into it and disappeared from view. He then hauled his boat inside the cave and waited. By the time Harald reached the cave the mouth was flooded and there was no sign of Swein. Harald searched the island for Swein but could not find him. He then searched the rocks around the island but could find no trace of Swein or his boat and so he concluded that either the boat must have sunk or Swein had escaped to some of the other islands. Harald then left Eller Holm and went off to search for Swein in the surrounding islands.

When Swein was certain that the coast was clear he left his own boat in the cave. He took a boat belonging to some monks who had a settlement on the island and rowed to Sanday. When he landed, he pushed off the small boat and let it drift around the island until it was wrecked. If Earl Harald found the wreckage of the boat he would assume that Swein and his companions had drowned.

Swein went to the home of one of his kinsmen called Bard, who agreed to keep him and his companions in hiding. Bard put them into a part of the house which was reached through a secret door. That night Jon Voeng, Earl Harald's steward, who was out searching for Swein arrived with six men. Bard received them well and put on a large fire to warm them. Jon was very embittered towards Swein and spoke of his mischievous dealings with the earls. He blamed Swein for all the troubles that had occurred on the islands and said that he was a truce breaker and faithful to no one. Jon also blamed Swein for breaking the peace with Earl Harald and said that there would never be peace in the islands until Swein was banished. Bard and some of Jon's companions tried to say a few words in Swein's defence, but Jon would not listen. Jon then went on to miscall Earl Erlend and said there was no loss in his death.

When Swein heard this he could no longer restrain himself, so he pushed down the stones that blocked the secret door, making a great noise. Jon heard Swein coming and ran from the house in his bare feet. There was a hard frost during the night and before Jon reached another house his feet were badly frost bitten and some of his toes fell off. Bard intervened on behalf of Jon's companions and Swein gave them peace. Swein stayed at the house all night. In the morning Bard gave Swein a boat and he sailed with his companions to South Ronaldsay where he hid in a cave. Sometimes he took his meals at a house ashore, but he always returned to the cave at night and was constantly on his guard for Earl Harald and his men.

One morning Swein saw a large ship sailing towards South Ronaldsay and immediately recognised it as one of Earl Rognvald's ships. The ship put in at South Ronaldsay and five of the crew went ashore. Swein and his men were standing on a headland and they threw stones at the men coming ashore. Swein then launched his boat and rowed towards the ship. When the boat was rowed past the ship, Swein was standing in the front holding a spear. Earl Rognvald held a shield to protect himself, but Swein did not throw the spear. The ship came so close inshore that it grounded on the sand. When Earl Rognvald knew that the ship had grounded he held up a truce shield. Seeing this, Swein told his men to row towards the ship, as his intention had always been to be at peace with Earl Rognvald.

They came ashore and held a conference and agreed very well. While they were talking they saw Earl Harald's ship sailing from Caithness to Walls. Rognvald told Swein to row over to Caithness if he wished to avoid Harald. Swein and Rognvald left South Ronaldsay at the same time: Swein sailed to Stroma while Rognvald went to the mainland of Orkney. Harald spotted Swein's boat and gave chase. On reaching Stroma, and knowing that he was being pursued by Harald, Swein left his boat and hid on the island. When Harald reached Stroma, he saw Swein's boat and suspecting that Swein and his followers had laid an ambush, would not go ashore. A man named Amundi, who was Harald's friend and also a relative of Swein, interceded between them and made a peace agreement. A gale arose and they had to stay on the island until it abated. Swein and Harald slept in the same bed and their men stayed in the same house.

Shortly after this event, Swein went to the Hebrides where he remained for some time. He then returned to the Orkneys, landing at

Rousay, and continued to Birsay where he stayed with Earl Rognvald until the spring. They were joined by Earl Harald who had just returned from the Shetlands. Rognvald arranged for the peace treaty between Harald and Swein to be renewed and a meeting was arranged in St Magnus Cathedral where the contract was confirmed.

Some time later, Swein received a message from Harald asking him to come to a meeting. At first Swein distrusted Harald, but finally agreed to attend. Harald and Thorbiorn Klerk were at the meeting place and Harald surprised Swein by restoring to him a scarlet tunic and a long ship which he had taken the previous winter. Harald told him that their friendship should never be dissolved. Swein was well pleased with the meeting and reported to Earl Rognvald who was delighted that at last there was peace between Swein and Harald.

On a subsequent plundering escapade Swein, Thorbiorn Klerk and Eirik sailed first to the Hebrides, then along the west coast as far as the Scilly Isles where they gained a great victory, returning to the Orkneys laden with booty.

After Earls Rognvald and Harald had made peace with Swein they were always together. Earl Rognvald was the ruler, but on the whole they got on very well together. After the expedition to the Scilly Isles, Thorbiorn Klerk became a counsellor to Earl Harald. Swein went to his home at Gairsay and lived in splendour on his loot.

Thorbiorn Klerk eventually fell out of favour with Earl Rognvald for his many acts of violence. Thorbiorn was outlawed for the murder of Thorarinn at an inn in Kirkwall and he sought refuge in Caithness with his brother-in-law Hosvir.

Swein went on further marauding raids, sailing along the west coast of Scotland where he was engaged in a sea battle with Sumarlida Hold, the Norse ruler of Argyle. Sumarlida had seven ships and the battle was very fierce, but in the end Sumarlida and many of his men were killed. Swein pursued Gillaodran, who commanded one of Sumarlida's ships, into one of the sea lochs and slew him and fifty men. He continued on his raid around the coast of Britain and in the autumn returned to Orkney, loaded with his spoils. He visited Earl Rognvald who was well pleased with his deeds.

Death of Earl Rognvald

Thorbiorn Klerk spent some of his time hiding in Caithness, but for the remainder visited the court of Malcolm, King of the Scots, with whom he was very friendly.

Every summer Earls Rognvald and Harald visited the forests of Caithness to hunt reindeer. When they landed at Thurso they were informed that Thorbiorn Klerk was in hiding in the vicinity with some men, and intended to attack them.

The Earls gathered one hundred men around them and set off for the forests in search of Thorbiorn. They slept the first night in a shieling. The next day they were passing through Calder and Earl Rognvald was riding ahead of the party. They came to a farm at North Calder in the parish of Halkirk where Hoskuld the farmer was building a corn stack. When he recognised Earl Rognvald he greeted him in a loud voice so that he could be heard some distance away. The corn stack was but a short distance from the house where Thorbiorn Klerk was sitting drinking. When Thorbiorn heard Hoskuld greet Earl Rognvald, he and his men grasped their arms and ran from the house. Earl Rognvald was sitting on his horse near the end of a passageway which led from the house. When Thorbiorn emerged from the house he struck a savage blow at Earl

Earl Rognvald is recognised by the farmer at Calder

Rognvald with his battle axe. One of Rognvald's retainers, named Asolf, tried to ward off the blow, but his hand was severed and the blow struck Earl Rognvald, inflicting a wound. Rognvald tried to jump from his horse, but his foot stuck in the stirrups. At that moment, one of Thorbiorn's men stabbed him with a spear and Thorbiorn wounded him again with his axe. Thorbiorn was speared by one of Rognvald's men and retreated behind the house. Then Harald and his men arrived and saw Thorbiorn behind the farm house. Harald's men wanted to pursue Thorbiorn but he dissuaded them saying that he would wait for Earl Rognvald's opinion, unaware that his friend was dying. Harald was then told that Rognvald had been killed by Thorbiorn Klerk.

By this time Thorbiorn Klerk and his men had got out on boggy moorland on the other side of the farm house. A mossy hag separated Thorbiorn's men and the Earl's followers. A battle ensued but the mossy hag, which was deep and broad, kept them apart and they could only throw spears and missiles at each other. Thorbiorn ordered his men not to respond and when Harald's men had exhausted their supply, he pleaded with Harald for his life to be spared. He said that Earl Rognvald had intended the same fate for him and Thorbiorn pleaded his case with many fair words. Harald began to listen to him, but his followers urged that the death of Rognvald should be avenged and no quarter should be given to Thorbiorn. Harald finally led his men across the moss hag and Thorbiorn's men were cut to pieces. When only nine were left alive Thorbiorn approached Harald and fell on his knees, begging for mercy. Harald told him:

"Save yourself Thorbiorn, for I have not the heart to kill you."

Thorbiorn and his men ran off to a deserted shieling at Assery, but were pursued by the Earl's party led by a man named Magnus. Thorbiorn and his men tried to fortify themselves in a cottage in the shieling, but Magnus set it on fire. The heat forced Thorbiorn and his men out of the building and although they defended themselves bravely they were all slain by Magnus and his men. When Thorbiorn Klerk slew Earl Rognvald, the words uttered by Swein when he was besieged by Rognvald and Thorbiorn in Lambaborg Castle, came true: "It is my foreboding that you will repay him (Earl Rognvald) worse for all the honour he has done to you before you part, for nobody will gain good fortune from any dealings with you." Earl Rognvald was killed on August 20th, 1158.

Earl Harald had Rognvald's body carried in great splendour across the Pentland Firth to South Ronaldsay where it was interred at a church. Many miracles were said to have taken place at his grave and for a long time after his death, the blood remained fresh on the stones where he was killed at North Calder. Earl Rognvald was canonised by the Pope in 1192 and his body exhumed and re-interred in St Magnus Cathedral, Kirkwall.

After Rognvald's death, Earl Harald took possession of the islands and became their sole ruler. His wife was named Afrika and they had four children, Heinrek, Hakon, Helena and Margaret. Swein and his wife Ingrid fostered Hakon when he was very young. When Hakon grew up, Swein took him on all his marauding raids and gave him every honour that he could bestow upon him. During the winters he lived with Swein's in Gairsay where eighty retainers were always kept. The drinking hall attached to the house was one of the largest in Europe at that time.

In the spring Swein sowed his crops and did a large amount of the work himself. After the work on the land was finished, he went off on a marauding raid with his ships, returning after midsummer. He called this raid 'spring viking'. After the corn was cut and the harvest secured, he went off on another raid which he called 'autumn viking'. He usually returned from this trip in the early winter before the storms started.

One spring Swein and young Hakon went on an expedition. With five ships they plundered the Hebrides. The inhabitants were so afraid of Swein that when they saw his ships approach they buried all their valuables, or hid them under a pile of stones. Swein took very little in the Hebrides and so he went south to the Isle of Man, but again he was seen by the natives who hid all their valuables. He therefore turned his attention to Ireland where he plundered several places and captured a large amount of valuable booty. He intercepted two English ships bound for Dublin, laden with cloth and other merchandise. Swein and his men took all the cargoes and left two crews with their ships and a small quantity of provisions. He then sailed to the Hebrides where he divided the booty among his men. When they sailed for Orkney, they covered the sails on all the ships with English cloth to give the impression that their sails were made of valuable material.

Swein went home to Gairsay with a large quantity of English wine and he prepared a magnificent banquet, inviting Earl Harald as one of his guests. While the feast was in progress there was a lot of talk about Swein's past exploits. Earl Harald finally said:

"I wish, Swein, you would now leave off your marauding expeditions; it is good now to drive home a whole wagon. You know that your plundering has fed you and your men for a long time, but to most men of violence it happens that they perish in their raiding, if they do not leave off in time."

Swein looked to the Earl and said, smiling:

"This is well said my Lord; you have spoken like a friend and it is good to take sound advice from you, but some complain that you are not an over just man yourself."

Earl Harald replied:

"I must be responsible for my own acts, but I spoke as it occurred to me." Swein said:

"Your intention is no doubt good my Lord, and it shall be so that I will discontinue my marauding expeditions, for I am getting old and my strength is wasting away in the wet work and the fighting. I am now going to make an autumn expedition, and I wish it to be no less glamorous than the spring one. Then I shall leave off war going."

The Earl replied:

"It is difficult to know which comes first – death or lasting fame."

The conversation ended there but before Harald left Gairsay, Swein gave him some valuable gifts and they parted on very good terms.

Swein's last expedition

Shortly after the banquet at Gairsay, Swein began preparing to go on a marauding expedition. He made extra special preparations for this expedition as it was to be his last, and he took seven longships, all well manned. Earl Harald's son, Hakon went with him. They sailed around the north-west coast of Scotland to the Hebrides where they made several raids, but they were very disappointed as they captured very little. Swein then sailed to Ireland, raiding the north coast and taking large amounts of booty. He decided to end his career as a pirate with a spectacular feat and so he sailed south to Dublin. Swein entered the city at night, taking the citizens by surprise. He plundered the city and captured the rulers. When the citizens knew that their rulers had been captured, they surrendered the city to Swein. They promised to pay him as much ransom money as he wished for the return of their leaders. He was to quarter his men in the city and have command of it, and this arrangement was sworn to by the Dublin men. Swein and his party returned to their ships for the night, but in the morning they were to take over the town and receive hostages from the people.

When Swein and his crew returned to their ships, the Dublin men held a secret meeting. They considered all the dangers and difficulties in which they were placed and thought it a terrible hardship that they should have to surrender their town to the most notorious pirate in the world. They were determined to save their city and so they decided to play false to Swein. Their plan was to dig large pits at the gates of the city and at other places where Swein and his men were likely to go. The pits were then disguised with a thin covering which would give way under the weight of a man. Straw was placed over the pits so that they could not be seen and armed men were hidden nearby.

Next morning Swein and his men rose early, armed themselves and walked towards the town. A large number of the inhabitants met him at the gates and Swein was very pleased, thinking that they were there to welcome him. He never suspected the real motive for them being there. The crowd were careful to stand on each side of the pit and in this way Swein and his men were forced to walk in to the trap. Swein, who was leading his men, stepped unsuspecting on to the slender covering, which immediately gave way plunging him and several of his companions into the pit. The armed Dublin men then emerged from their hiding place and fell upon the pirates. A fierce battle ensued and although Swein and his men were greatly outnumbered they put up a terrific fight. Inevitably, they were overcome and all were slain. Swein was the last to die, but before he fell he uttered these words:

"Know all men, whether I die today or not, that I am the holy Earl Rognvald's henchman, and my confidence is where he is with God."

Thus ended the life of Swein, who is described in the *Sagas* as being the greatest man in the Western Lands, either in olden times or at the present day. The date of Swein's death is believed to be 1160.

The surviving members of Swein's expedition were able to leave Dublin and return to Orkney. After Swein's death, his estates were divided between his two sons, Olaf and Andres. They shared the house and drinking hall at Gairsay and it is believed that they enlarged it. Andres married Frida who was sister to Bishop Bjarni.

Swein lived by violence and died by violence, but he had extraordinary skill and courage which elevated him to a special place in history. He lived in a very tough period in our history and was a man respected by King, Earls and commoners alike, so he must have possessed special characteristics which were not entirely those of a violent freebooter, as he is generally known. Piracy was the general trade of the Norsemen at that time, so it can be said that Swein was more than a good tradesman. If he had directed his talents to any other type of work, there can be no doubt that he would have been a great success.

REFERENCES

The Orkneyinga Saga Translated from the Icelandic by Jon A. Hjaltalin & Gilbert Goudie, Edited by Joseph Anderson. Edinburgh. 1873

Civil and Traditional History of Caithness from the 10th century by James T. Calder. Wick 1887.